# FAIRIES AND HONEY

Grey Liliy

ISBN-13: 978-1943161058
ISBN-10: 1943161054

Cover Design by Grey Liliy

# CHAPTER 1

"SO YOUR NAME is Harold," Diana said, her plastic smile straining the edges of her cheeks. The ice in her glass clacked together as the pieces stuck to one another split apart, melting in the summer heat. "And you're dressed like a bee."

"Yes," Harold answered. "A honey bee."

The two long antennae bounced as he spoke. Impressed at how well he had hidden the headband under his hair, Diana wondered what he had done to accomplish it. You could barely tell it was there. The black sclera contact lenses were also rather impressive. Diana couldn't think of anyone she knew who wore those things, in any color, let alone black. They were creepy, though. He blinked, drawing attention to them, and Diana resisted the urge to jump out of her chair and sprint for the hills.

"I'm sorry I didn't mention that part in the dating profile. I've found listing you work for a Queen tends to attract the wrong sort of company." Harold leaned forward conspiratorially and smiled, "Gold diggers. They think they can get free honey, you know?"

Diana had been thinking the reason Harold didn't list his bee getup on his profile had been more along the lines of "Admitting I like to walk around in a honey bee costume keeps people from taking my profile seriously" than gold digging, but she at least had the slightest impression Harold believed what he was saying.

Unless that had been some sort of joke.

Diana watched his smile falter as she failed to react. Of course that had been a joke. She folded her napkin under the table and winced as she glanced at his costume again. Or Diana hoped that it had been a joke. She honestly couldn't tell right now, and that was a tad worrisome.

She picked her glass off the table and took a polite sip to avoid answering his comment. Twenty minutes. She promised herself she would give every blind date twenty minutes to avoid judging a book by its cover or something. Harold fidgeted with the fluffy fur collar on his throat and Diana took a deeper drink from her glass.

Maybe she could break that promise just this once and give him fifteen minutes. The man was dressed like a honey bee, for goodness sake!

Harold had gone the whole nine yards, too. In addition to the very life-like antennae that sprouted out from behind his golden blond bangs and the sclera contacts that covered the entire whites of his eyes, Harold also had donned: The aforementioned fluffy, furry throat collar in cream, a matching slick, metallic shirt with plain black sleeves, and his pants were gold and black striped. The crowning glory was a pair of clear metallic wings, held together by carefully crafted thick black veins made of some sort of rough, tar-like, material to hold their shape. The wings were currently draped over the back of Harold's chair like a cape.

At least he was dedicated to the delusion, Diana would give the man that.

"You work in a yogurt shop, right?" Harold asked after a few awkward moments of Diana's staring, clearly trying to change the subject. His voice was hoarse and had a bit of grit to it. Gravelly. It was an odd contrast to the whole "bee" thing he had going on. Diana half expected his voice to be high pitched and whiny when she had first sat down, but the rusty voice fit him somehow nonetheless. Harold held his hand up and mimicked pulling down a lever. "One of those soft serve places where you weigh it and pick your own toppings?"

"Yup," Diana said, gently setting her glass down. At least he was nice, and his face wasn't too bad either. Greek nose, diamond face. Average looking, but handsome in his own way. Diana imagined if he took out the contacts and ditched the costume, he might clean up pretty nice. Diana licked the side of her teeth. "That's my day. Swapping out toppings and cleaning out soft serve yogurt machines."

"You don't sound like you enjoy your work all that much." Harold laughed, coughing a second later as if the action had hurt his throat. Diana held her head up higher and almost asked if he was alright when Harold held up his hand. He reached over for a honey packet and dumped an extra helping of it into his tea. Diana figured that was his third one, not that she had meant to keep count. Harold sipped from the cup, and his throat did sound a little better, though it kept it's gravely edge. "Sorry, I'm okay. Just not used to laughing much lately."

*Probably more used to being laughed at,* Diana thought with a hint of pity.

She took a quick glance at her watch and noted the ten minute mark had ticked by. Harold officially had ten more minutes to prove he was worth the evening. Diana laced her fingers on the outdoor table, resting her hands in the middle of the day menu. "Can't say it's exactly mentally stimulating, no."

"What would you rather be doing?" Harold asked, polite and neat. The wind ruffled the fur on his collar, and he played with the edge of his menu, dragging thin, boney fingers along the edge while waiting for Diana's answer.

Diana crossed her legs under the table, and bit the edge of her lip as she tried to think of an answer. Harold waiting patiently, not judging, but still looking ridiculous with those antennae on his head and that furry collar. She laughed, and covered her mouth to hide the embarrassed smile. "I don't know. I guess if I did, I wouldn't be working at the yogurt shop."

"Fair enough," Harold said.

Diana checked her watch. Eight minutes left.

Awkward silence fell over the table as Harold shifted in his seat. Diana had no idea what to say to the man, and he seemed hesitant to bring up another topic. He rolled his shoulders, stretching them out like something was jabbing him in the middle of his spine.

Diana glanced at Harold's back, thinking she may have figured out the culprit for his discomfort. She waved a finger toward the glossy wings as they shifted and swayed behind Harold. "Those look heavy."

"Not really." Harold glanced over his shoulder and tugged at the side of one, pulling it up. The sunlight danced over the glossy surface, and he dropped it back into place a second later. "I barely notice them, really."

"Then what was wrong?" Diana asked, motioning to the way he'd been stretching with her own arms. "Shoulders hurt?"

"I slept wrong last night, that's all," Harold said.

"Right."

Mr. Honey Bee had five minutes left on the clock, and Diana struggled to find some way to fill the time. The man wasn't bad, but he wasn't exactly what Diana was looking for either. Even without the bee costume, there was nothing that she could see clicking between the two of them.

Diana flipped the menu upside-down and tried to remember how many dollar bills she had in her wallet. If she wasn't going to order anything from the cafe, she should still leave a tip to cover the table time and the drink she'd ordered. Right? Right.

Harold looked at his menu, drawing his finger down the items on the list as he read each one quietly aloud. He stopped at one and tilted his head. "I wonder if their baklava is any good."

And he picked the honey drenched dessert for lunch.

"You know Harold, I'm sorry, but I don't think this is going to work out." Diana grabbed her clutch purse and fished out a few single dollars and a ten to throw on the table. She was cutting his time short by two minutes, but Diana felt no one would hold it against her for breaking her rule just this once. "But thanks for meeting with me, and good luck on your future blind dates. Have a dessert on me."

"Diana?" Harold asked, looking up from the menu. "We haven't even ordered yet."

"I'm sorry," Diana said, the words practiced. The third time was supposed to the charm, and he was the oddest one yet. Diana had no idea things could get weirder than blind date number two and his obsession with onion rings. "I'm usually pretty good at figuring out if there's going to be a connection or not after a few minutes. This isn't going to go anywhere, and I hate leading people on."

"Oh, okay." Harold dropped his shoulders, and his eyes grew wide. Diana whistled internally. *Those are some nice contacts.* Even with his eyes open at their widest, she couldn't spot a speck of white. Harold rubbed his forearm through his sleeve and dropped his head. "Thanks for coming."

"For real, you're a good guy and I just know that you're going to find someone great just for you," Diana said, tapping her knuckles on the table top. "So go ahead and order that dessert and keep your head up."

"I'll try," Harold said. He waved his hand back and forth, his arm close to his chest. "Good luck to you, too."

Diana nodded and waved back as she stepped away from the table. She left Harold alone in his seat as she went to the fence gate at the edge of the outdoor square. The wind picked up, blowing her hair behind her and Diana glared at the weather as rain clouds began to head her way in the distance. Perfect. Bad date came with bad weather. At least the outdoor portion of the cafe was covered so Harold wouldn't get wet. The gate closed behind her just as the waiter showed up to greet Harold, and she blew out a breath of relief when he put her offer to good use and pointed at the menu where she'd seen the desserts.

Crisis averted, Diana slipped on a pair of sunglasses and started her quick walk to the car. Looked like it was another night alone with a tub of frozen yogurt and a good action movie.

# CHAPTER 2

DIANA DASHED ACROSS the west side of the outdoor mall's main traffic strip, dodging in and out of customers as they milled about their business. The clock in the center square said it was ten until ten, but Diana knew that thing was five minutes fast. She had plenty of time to get to work before they opened, even if it was a sixteen minutes sprint from where she was to her shop.

She wasn't late! Not this time!

"Stupid alarm clock," Diana hissed as she dodged another mall patron in her rush to work. It didn't help the parking garage was on the opposite end of the store where she worked. So far away from the cars, it was no wonder their foot traffic suffered all the time. She pulled the bill of her uniform hat down to keep it from blowing off in the wind as she turned the corner. "Can't believe I forgot to set it."

Her frozen yogurt shop was one more row down. All she had to do was get in the door before they opened and everything would be fine. Their boss never showed up until ten or twenty minutes after store open, and Diana had full confidence that Jolie could set up shop for business alone. Or at least she had texted as much when she woke Diana this morning with a lovely message of "Where are you?"

Diana groaned and picked up her pace as she heard the center clock chime in the background. She was so close! A few more miniature blocks and she'd be home free!

"Ow!" Diana shouted as she smacked into a firm wall.

She backed up a few paces and held her nose, glad she didn't fall over. She heard someone ask, "Are you okay?" and realized her wall had been a person.

"I am so sorry! I was in a rush and wasn't looking where I was going," Diana said. She looked up and met a pair of black eyes and stopped dead in her tracks. "Harold?"

"Diana," Harold answered. His honey bee costume was still in place, and he shuffled in his black boots as Diana gaped at him. He pointed at the logo at her shirt. "I didn't realize the yogurt place you worked was here at the mall."

"You didn't ask," Diana said. She clutched the strap of her purse and looked Harold over. No one seemed to be giving him a second glance as he stood in the middle of the busy sidewalk dressed up in a bee costume. Surely he should be getting a least one or two odd glances? "Here shopping?"

"No, I'm working," Harold answered.

He pointed next to him and Diana turned to follow his finger. She looked up at the giant black and yellow sign and put her hand on her hip. The sign had a giant cartoon bee hugging the first letter of the store name. Diana blinked, "You work at the honey store?"

"Yup," Harold said, scratching the back of his hair. He turned and waved at some kids with a bright smile as they passed and they waved right back. "I've been working here for about a year now."

"So the thing about working for a Queen was a joke?" Diana asked, and Harold nodded. She looked in the shop window and saw at least ten or more tables covered in shelves of honey jars. In the back there was some larger stands that looked full, but she couldn't see what was back there. "Now I feel dumb for not picking up on that, but I'm also sort of shocked I've never seen you out here before."

"I'm not surprised," Harold answered, rubbing the side of his face just under a black colored contact lens. He leaned on the small sample table that had been set up next to the door entrance. Small packets of honey were spread out along with business cards for the store. "I mostly work inside, and we're sort of a speciality shop. If you're not looking to find a new local honey brand or beekeeping equipment, you don't really have a lot of reason to be around the store that often."

"So you guys sell honey you collect yourselves?" Diana asked, ready to distract herself from not noticing the guy dressed like a bee for a year. There had to at least have been rumors, even if she had missed the stupid shop for this long! "Bet that's a lot of work."

"Oh, no," Harold said, waving his hand back and forth. "The boss doesn't have any beekeeping farms herself. She just loves honey and wants to support all the local beekeepers. So she made a store front for all of them to sell their goods, and then she orders equipment wholesale for them. The boss also has a bunch of how-to books and stuff for sale, too, if people want to start their own farms. And sometimes we sell kids toys and candy during the holidays."

Diana looked over his bee costume again and then back at the shop. Maybe he wore that outfit to the date because he had just come from work, and was embarrassed about it? "Why the mascot costume, though? This doesn't seem like the store that would need one."

"I said I worked here, not that I was the mascot," Harold said, digging the tip of his boot into the pavement. He reached up and tugged at one of his two antennae, rolling it between two fingers. He avoided her eye contact, staring hard at the ground. "It's not a costume. It's how I dress."

And now he was embarrassed. *Good going, Diana.* She grit her teeth together and felt awful watching his face drop.

"Well, at least you're working at a place that appreciates it," Diana said, hoping to at least cover a fraction of the damage she'd just caused.

*Work.*

Diana looked through the store window and zeroed in on a wall clock. She cursed under her breath and waved to Harold. "Speaking, I'm late for work myself! Bye!"

"Bye," Harold said, waving. "Have a good day."

"You, too!" Diana answered before she could help herself.

She dashed around the corner and picked up her pace until she was full on sprinting through the outdoor mall. So, Harold worked in the same place she did. Diana looked up at the sky and made a vow to start paying more attention. If she'd been working at the mall this long and never noticed there was a man in a full honey bee costume hanging around inside or outside one of the shops, she needed to get her act together.

After passing three more shop fronts, Diana slowed her pace to a brisk walk. No reason to upset any of her own possible patrons by dashing into the store like a mess. She pushed into the door and nodded at Jolie behind the counter before quickly heading to the back storage room and dumping off her things. Diana washed her hands, adjusted her uniform and joined Jolie back in the front.

"Not like you to be late," Jolie said the second Diana got behind the serving counter. "You're lucky the boss isn't here yet."

"Alarm clock didn't go off," Diana said. "Sorry."

"Eh, it happens," Jolie shrugged. She winked and shoved at Diana's shoulder. "Secret's safe with me!"

"Good." Diana smiled and turned her attention back to work. Just another day helping people find the perfect frozen treat. Joy!

"Three strikes means you're out," Jolie said, popping a large bubble from her chewing gum. The girl leaned on the cashier counter, flicking the pens in the cup next to the register. "Three outs and you've got to switch from defense to offense, and I just don't think you're cut out for that."

"It's blind dating, not baseball," Diana answered, tugging over the toppings refill cart. She shoved it between the two serving counters and began the tedious process of topping off each mini tub on the only open lane. Diana still wasn't sure why they had a second line when it hadn't been opened once since she'd started working there. "And I highly doubt I'll find the winner even after ten or twenty dates. That's the point of blind dating! To see a bunch of guys to find just one."

"Guess so," Jolie said. She popped another bubble and groaned as she turned around and crossed her arm on the counter. Her hair spilled over her shoulders from her ponytail as she buried her hand in her arms. Jolie mumbled, "Least you've got time. You're only twenty-two. You've got years yet to find a guy out of those hundreds you seem content to see one at a time at random."

"I get the picture," Diana said, flicking an almond at Jolie's head. She leaned on the serving bar and sighed at the empty shop. Three o'clock in the afternoon and the place was dead. Not a customer in sight for miles to distract her from this conversation. Diana dumped a scoop of chocolate sprinkles into a tub, wiping up the few that escaped with a napkin. "You think the blind dating is stupid?"

"Not stupid," Jolie answered, face still buried in her arms. "The odds just aren't in your favor. There's no way you're going to get a guy to meet your standards when you're only giving him twenty minutes."

Diana huffed, and jabbed the scoop back into the larger container. She twisted the cap back onto the large jug with a vicious twist of her hand. "I regret telling you anything about how the dates went."

"No you don't," Jolie said, popping her head up. "You love telling me every little detail about your life."

Jolie hopped off the counter and stretched her arms up over her head, stepping up on her tip-toes as she arched her back, cracking her spine. Jolie dropped her arms at her sides, her heels smacking into the checkered floor tiles in her slip-on shoes. Diana tapped her toe on the ground, ignoring Jolie as she fixed her mini skirt and adjusted her logo polo top.

Diana knew the interrogation was coming even before Jolie skipped down the serving line and grabbed the handle of the topping cart. She put a foot on the bottom shelf, and pushed up to stand on the cart. "So spill. What was so bad about guy number three that you almost went running at ten minutes?"

"He was dressed like a bee," Diana said, setting her foot on the other end of the cart shelf to keep it from falling over. "Do I really need another reason?"

"So he was a creep?" Jolie asked, swaying back and forth on the cart. "Some kind of pervert?"

Diana half wondered if Jolie knew who Diana was talking about. What were the odds there were two people in town who dressed like a bee? Though if Diana hadn't noticed the guy worked at the mall, maybe Jolie hadn't either. She was sort of obsessed with baseball to the point she blocked out most other things.

Unless it was Diana's love life. Then Jolie was all gossip.

With a valid question.

Diana rested her chin on her hand, and thought back to the date two nights ago. Harold had been soft spoken, and rather shy. He asked about Diana's interests in the few minutes she'd given him, and barely said anything about himself aside from the joke. Diana had been a little unsettled about the bee costume thing, sure, but the lack of self-confidence and his unknown profession were equal factors in the decision to leave at the eighteen minute mark.

But she really couldn't call the guy creepy, outside of the contacts anyway.

"Nah, he didn't give off any bad vibes of that sort," Diana said, finally. She rolled her finger in the air and shrugged. "He was a little weird, but he didn't strike me as dangerous or anything."

"Weird can be good," Jolie said. She scrunched her nose and stepped off the cart. She reached over the counter and pulled back a napkin, shoving her old gum in it, and rolled it up into a ball. Jolie put her hands up like she was ready to pitch a baseball, and threw the wadded up gum toward the trash can across the store. The napkin hit the rim and landed properly inside the plastic bag. Jolie gave a thumbs up and said, "You know?"

"Maybe I should call him up again and introduce you," Diana said, smiling. She shook her head and tugged the cart back out into the main aisle and toward the back room. "You're obsessed with baseball, and he thinks he's a bee. Perfect match."

"Nah," Jolie winked. She swung an invisible bat in the air, her arms moving in a practiced swing. "I've got cleanup hitter in my sights right now. He's the only guy on the team who can hit my pitches."

"Sounds like quite the catch," Diana said.

"Hey! Only I'm allowed to make baseball puns," Jolie said, putting her hands on her hips. The frown on her face was a genuine mix of irritation and pride that scrunched her nose at the bridge. "That's my job."

"No, your job is to watch the register," Diana said, nodding her head toward the front door. A couple had just arrived and was about to pull on the handle. Thank goodness for customers. "Come on, happy faces."

"Yeah, yeah," Diana said. She spun on her heel and waved her hand as the bell over the door rang. "Hi! Welcome! Welcome! I hope you guys are in the mood for some delicious frozen yogurt!"

Diana shut the back room door, and put on her best customer service grin as Jolie explained how they charged per yogurt cup to the new patrons.

"I think failed date number three is waiting outside the door," Jolie said, popping a piece of bubblegum into her mouth.

The store was due to close in ten minutes and the lobby was empty. Halfway through an early cleanup, Diana placed the box of plastic wrap on the countertop behind her and looked at the door. Sure enough, Harold stood outside the store entrance, fidgeting in place. He watched the ground, and rubbed his hands together.

"Should I tell him to go away?" Jolie whispered. She leaned next to Diana as conspiratorially as an alarm clock, and pointed widely at the door. "That's him right? The honey bee guy?"

"No, I'll go see what he wants," Diana said. She wiped her hands on her jean skirt and scooted around the counter. She pushed open the other half of the french doors, and poked her head out. "Did you need something, Harold? If you want some yogurt, we're still open for another ten minutes."

"No, that's fine. I just wanted to ask you something." Harold rubbed the side of his arm, pinching at the black sleeves. Diana wished she could tell where his eyes were looking, but the contacts hid his gaze well. Harold bit the side of his lip. "I wasn't sure if I should wait until the store closed or not to bother you."

"You can ask now," Diana said, glancing at her grinning coworker. She took a step outside and gently closed the door behind her. No reason Jolie needed to hear this all first hand. She was already staring at them through the window, and that girl had enough ammo already. Diana waved at the store behind her. "There's no customers right now."

"Okay," Harold said. He dropped his sleeve and held his hands at his side, his posture stiff and unsure. Diana crossed her arms as she waited for him to collect himself. It took him a moment, but Harold eventually asked, "Would you like to go out again? I know the first date didn't go so well, but I was wondering if we could, maybe if you want to, try again?"

"I'm not sure," Diana said, looking to the side. Harold looked so damn hopeful, but she also really hated leading people on. It was the entire point of the twenty minute rule in the first place. If she didn't like a guy immediately, she probably was never going to like him. However, Diana did find herself a little curious despite it all. She tapped her fingers on her arm, and shifted her weight to her hip. "What made you ask again?"

"After you left the cafe, I figured we were never going to see each other again," Harold said, grabbing the bottom of his shirt. His wings fluttered a bit under a gust of wind, and he reached back to grab them before they flapped too hard. His antennae, on the other hand, continued to wave back and forth in the breeze. "But then we ran into each other this morning, and I couldn't help but think that it was a sign I should take another chance."

The logic wasn't horrible.

Diana rubbed the back of her neck, and bit her lip. She did sort of leave him fairly quickly that night, and if she was being honest, she gave up on him around the ten minute mark instead of his full twenty. Diana concentrated on the tip of his wing near the ground. Did she want to give Mr. Honey Bee another chance? Or should she just shut this down now before he got his hopes up? Diana groaned inside. Maybe she should just give up on dating. This was the part where she always fell apart.

"It's okay if you don't want to," Harold added quickly. He swallowed and started to rub the back of his thumb. He watched the ground, and she noticed his breathing had picked up. The heavy breaths moved the fur around his collar and shirt. "I just thought I'd ask, but I understand if you want to say no."

"She says yes," Jolie said, popping her head out the door. She blew a bubble out of her gum, and nodded her head toward Diana. "You were asking her out right? She says yes."

"Jolie!" Diana hissed, turning her head toward the traitor. "What are you doing?"

"I was about to close up the store, but you're still out here with Mr. Third Blind Date," Jolie said. She waved him up and down and shrugged. "You said he wasn't a creep, so it's not like he's really struck out yet. It won't kill you to give him another chance at bat."

Diana groaned, rubbing between her eyes. "That's not the point, Jolie."

"Then what is?" Jolie asked. She held her hand out and said, "Nice to meet you in person, Mr. Third Blind Date."

"Ah, likewise," Harold answered, a dusting of red showing up on his cheeks. He took her hand and shook it. "Nice to meet you, Ms. Jolie."

"See? He's nice." Jolie gave a thumbs up. "And he's the first guy to ask you out since you started the whole online dating thing in the first place, so you really have no reason to say no."

"Harold, can you give me one second?" Diana sucked in a breath, and shook her head. She grabbed Jolie in a headlock and kicked open the store door. She dragged her laughing friend back inside the store and dumped her in the nearest table seat. "Stay out of my love life."

"You wanted to tell him yes, you're just scared," Jolie said, her lip quirking in a smile. "It was written all over your face from the glass outside."

Diana stopped. "What are you talking about?"

"I know he's the first guy you said didn't give you bad vibes. Two, like I said, he's the first guy to ask you out, and I know that makes you happy," Jolie said, sticking her legs out. She crossed her ankles and watched Harry in the window. Diana followed her gaze, trying to keep Harold in sight without turning her head and making it obvious. In the meantime,

Jolie went in for the kill with her final justification. "Besides, the guy's cute. Can't go wrong there. I mean it's a date, so it's not like you're going out there and marrying the guy."

"Fine, fine. You've got a point." Diana rubbed her face, and watched Jolie from between her fingers. She gave up on trying to hide her spying, and turned just enough back toward the front of the store to see Harold waiting on the other side of the glass. He bit his lip, and it was sort of cute. In a childish kind of way. Diana dropped her hands. "One more date can't hurt."

"That's the spirit!" Jolie threw her fist in the air. "Go get him!"

Diana trotted back outside, and immediately apologized for leaving Harold outside and alone like that. He waved it off, and Diana steeled herself for what she hoped wasn't a mistake. "You know what? She's got a point. Sure, we can go out again if you want to."

"Really?" Harold asked, smiling brightly. Diana's heart skipped a beat at the joyful expression. When was the last time a man had looked at her that way? Harold continued grinning, and his shoulders popped back. Standing straight, Diana had to look up to keep eye contact. When Harold wasn't slouching, he was at least four inches taller than her. "That's great! Where would you like to go?"

"Any place is fine," Diana said, rubbing her elbow. She dragged a foot across the ground, hiding it behind her ankle. If she was going to shake things up, might as well shake them up! Diana shrugged. "Why don't I meet you at the mall clock at seven tomorrow, and you can surprise me."

"Alright." Harold put his hands in his pockets and leaned back. He nodded. "I can do that."

"Great," Diana said. "So, I guess I'll see you then?"

"Definitely!" Harold said. He continued grinning like a fool, and it must have been a contagious smile, because Diana felt the same tugging at her corner lip. "I'll be sure to dress up for it!"

Did that mean he was going to ditch the costume? Diana was about to ask what he meant, when another girl came around the corner and marched up to Harold.

"Harry!" The girl hissed, smacking him hard in the arm. She towered over him, at least a foot taller, and Harold backed away from her. Diana glanced at the name tag on her honey-colored t-shirt and read the name "Princess." She put her hands-on her hips and asked, "Why did you run off? I've been looking everywhere for you!"

"I was on break, and I was going to be right back," Harold said, folding back in on himself. His bright smile turned sheepish and he pulled his hands out his pockets. "I just wanted to say hello to Diana."

"Isn't that the name of the girl who ditched you on that date a couple days ago?" Princess asked, glaring over at Diana. She curled her lip up and flicked her loose, dark hair over her shoulder. "Why would you want to say hello to her?"

"She didn't ditch me," Harold mumbled, his cheeks getting redder by the second. "I told you that."

"You ditched him," Princess said, poking Diana's shoulder. Her green eyes were full of accusation, and she huffed loudly. The overdramatic reactions didn't impress Diana in the slightest, and gave her the impression Princess was younger than she looked. "I don't care what you call it. What sort of person runs out on a date before you even order the food?"

"It's not my fault the cafe was slow," Diana mumbled. Her twenty minute rule usually left plenty of time to at least start eating before things could turn sour. Food did wonders for keeping her in the seat past the mark. "And what business is it of yours?"

"Harry's my friend and you hurt his feelings," Princess answered. She reached up and curled a strand of brown hair around her finger and smirked. "What more reason do I need?"

"Come on," Harold said, tugging on Princess' sleeve. "She just said yes to another date, so please leave Diana alone."

"Whatever," Princess said. She grabbed Harold's arm and tugged him away from Diana and the yogurt shop. "We've got to clean up early today so mommy can get to her doctor's appointment on time."

Harold kept his eyes on Diana as he was dragged around the corner. His wings and antennae bounced, as his arm waved back and forth. "I'll see you tomorrow!"

"Bye," Diana said, waving back. She stuck her hands on her hips and looked at the sky. "He's going to dress up, huh?"

Diana locked the front store doors with her mind reviewing the outfits in her closet. She laughed, rubbing the back of her neck. "Look at me, getting ready already for a date for a guy who likes to dress like a bee. Who would have thought it?"

She dutifully ignored Jolie's answer of "Me!"

# CHAPTER 3

CONSIDERING THEY BOTH worked in an outdoor mall, Diana felt fairly confident that she wouldn't need anything fancier than a skirt and some heels. Neither one of them could probably afford a place that required black tie, so Diana felt pretty safe with dress casual. It was always better to be overdressed than under, anyway, so if they ended up at fast food she would still look good. If she was going to make up for ditching on Harold early, she should at least give him a real chance this time and put her best foot forward.

For the date, Diana had chosen her favorite outfit: A knee-length green sun dress with a medium sized sunflower broach pinned at the base of one of the straps. Her heeled sandals were a reasonable two inches tall, and Diana had found a black clutch for her purse. Since the broach was enough jewelry on its own, Diana had forgone a necklace, but did manage to find a cute pair of fairy stud earrings to match. Her hair was up in a bun, and her makeup was perfect. All in all, Diana felt pretty confident in the ensemble she'd chosen for the date.

She texted the outfit to Jolie and got a thumbs up in response, so that was a nice confidence boost, too.

Diana arrived at the clock tower at ten minutes to seven, right on time. She checked the time on her phone from her clutch, and glanced around the area for a man with honey blond hair. Diana wondered if she'd recognize Harold outside of his bee costume if he did decide to ditch it. Not seeing anyone who looked like they'd fit the bill, Diana shoved her phone back in her purse and attempted to be patient.

"Sorry to keep you waiting," Harold said, tapping her shoulder from the back.

Diana turned and snapped her mouth shut mid greeting.

Harold hadn't been kidding when he said he was going to dress up. The contacts, antennae, wings, and fur collar were still present, but he'd traded out the metallic shirt for a black collared button-up and a golden-yellow vest. His slacks were black with yellow pinstripes, and he'd traded the boots for a nice pair of dress shoes. To finish off his look, Harold had a honeycomb barrette clipped to the side of his hair just behind the antennae. Harold was still dressed like a honey bee, but he did clean up nice with the crisp lines of his suit showing off his lanky figure.

"Hey there," Diana said after finding her voice. She shoved a loose strand of hair behind her ear and smiled. "I wasn't waiting long, don't worry about it."

"Ah, good," Harold said. He placed a hand on his stomach and visibly relaxed, with his shoulders dropping and a soft smile sneaking on his face. "Princess wouldn't stop fussing with my suit, so I was running a little late."

"She was the girl who came and got you yesterday, right?" Diana asked. She held her clutch under her arm and tapped the side of her cheek. "She didn't seem to like me very much."

"Princess doesn't like a lot of people," Harold said, his cheeks crinkling in an amused smile. He was grinning like Princess was his own personal inside joke, and Diana couldn't help but feel her own lip twitch. The amusement was contagious. "That's why her mom makes her work in the back instead of in the front of the store on the bad days."

"Her mom owns the store?" Diana paused and flashed back to something he'd said earlier. "Why would she be helping you get ready, anyway? Do you two live near each other?"

"I live in the attic apartment above her house," Harold explained. He straightened out his vest and pressed his lips together. "So I see her and her mother all the time outside of work."

"Fun," Diana said while thinking the exact opposite. If that was what the daughter was like, Diana never wanted to meet the mom. She straightened her dress out, and addressed something she'd noticed the other day. "She calls you 'Harry', right?"

"Yeah," Harold said, tugging on the end of an antennae. "Most of my friends call me that."

Diana tapped her fingers on her purse. "And you said Princess was a friend, so I guess that makes sense."

"You can, you can call me that too if you want," Harold added. "I mean, I was going to tell you that anyway. I don't usually go by my full name that often."

"Alright, from here on out it'll be Harry then." Diana clicked her tongue and decided that was enough talk about other girls, especially ones as prickly as Princess. "So, where are you taking me tonight?"

"You said I should surprise you, so that's what I'm going to do," Harry said. He held out his arm, bent at the elbow. Diana didn't see much harm in it, and wrapped her arm around the offered appendage. She was surprised to feel rather firm muscles through the fabric, and was curious how fit the rest of him might be. Harry began walking, and she kept pace easily enough, despite his long stride. "I hope you don't mind if we take my car, but it's about a fifteen minute drive away and I don't want to spoil the surprise."

"That's alright," Diana said. "My car's in the employee lot, so I'm not worried about anyone touching it."

And she had Jolie on speed dial, just in case the honey bee turned out to be a wasp in disguise.

"Great," Harry confirmed. The brilliant smile from yesterday made yet another appearance, and Diana found herself staring at it. Harry had a few teeth out of place on the bottom row, but there was still a nice charm to his toothy grin. He sucked in a breath and she could feel his muscles relax under her hold. "This should be fun."

Diana hummed in agreement, and let him lead her out to the main parking garage. The walk was quiet and nice, with most of the mall shops closed for the evening. Harry's car turned out to be a sensible little four door sedan, black with yellow accents, and he opened the passenger door for Diana to slip in. She covered her mouth with her hand to avoid laughing as Harry took much longer to get into the driver's seat, taking great care to avoid squashing or bending his wings on anything. But the material they were made from turned out to be rather flexible, and they curved neatly around him in the seat.

"Ready?" Harry asked, checking his rearview and side mirrors. He snapped on his seatbelt, and waited for Diana to do the same before turning the key to the ignition.

She gave him points for being safety conscious, and crossed one leg over the other as they pulled out of the parking lot. Honestly, so far the date was going fairly well, and it had only been ten minutes. Once you got over the shock of his costume, Harry was pretty nice when you got down to it. Diana typed a quick text to Jolie to let her know that if Diana didn't text again in thirty minutes to come looking, and then settled in for a nice drive down the back roads behind the mall.

"Why am I not surprised there are going to be flowers?" Diana chuckled, tapping Harry in the arm with her purse. The attendant behind the glass laughed at the two of them, and Harry ducked his head in embarrassment. He finished paying the entrance fee, waving as they walked away from the smiling ticket-taker. Diana took her ticket from Harry's hand with a grin, flipping the small piece of paper over to read the operation hours printed on the back. "Then again, a garden exhibit is better than a bee farm or something."

"That was my back up plan," Harry said, handing his ticket to the women at the entrance. The whole process reminded her more of going to a carnival than a garden, but she supposed it was one way to make sure people paid to get in. Diana followed suit, and both tickets were ripped and stubs were returned. Harry opened the glass door for Diana, and she passed through with ease. The lights in the green house were tinted blue, and it gave the whole area a lovely glow. "Though most beekeepers don't allow company after dark."

"I'm surprised the gardens are open," Diana said, her arms behind her back. She looked up at the large glass dome that encompassed them, seeing bits of glass shine under the lights. The greenhouse gravel crunched under her shoes, and the path winded neatly around well kept flower beds. Each plant had a little sign that stated its name and a few fun facts. "Didn't think night exhibits would be that popular."

"They're not," Harry said. He stopped and squatted next to a small ground-cover exhibit, crossing his arms over his knees. The ends of his wings curved as they stretched out behind him on the ground. Diana was careful not to step on them as she leaned over his shoulder and grinned at the bed of Hen and chicks. He poked the edge of a leaf and shrugged. "I thought it'd be nicer in here if it were less crowded."

"You're not wrong," Diana said, looking around the expanse of the greenhouse. Toward the back of the long building, she saw a few more sets of double doors and other than herself and Harry, there was no one else here. She tugged on the edge of his antennae before walking away.

"Come on, there's lots to see, isn't there?"

"Y-yeah," Harry said, hopping up from the ground. A light dusting of pink appeared on his cheeks, and his eyes kept to the flower bed. He wrapped his fingers around the same antennae and swallowed. "Though I imagine we'll see most of it after dinner. Our reservation is at eight."

"Dinner?" Diana asked.

"The back of the greenhouse opens up into the rest of the gardens. They have four more outdoor exhibits, and a large restaurant in the back." Harry caught up to Diana and stayed by her side as they followed the path toward the back doors. "I thought dinner would be nice, unless you already ate?"

"No worries," Diana chuckled. She popped out her phone and sent an "It's all okay" message to Jolie before putting it up for the evening. Diana was pretty sure at this point she wasn't going to need it. "Just a light snack in case your date night didn't involve food."

Harry pushed open the back greenhouse door and held it for her to pass through. Once on the other side he pointed toward the gravel path on the left. "The restaurant is just this way. We'll be a little early, but I don't think it'll matter."

"Not expecting a large wait?" Diana asked, raising an eyebrow. "You said you made reservations."

"Just in case." Harry twisted the end of his antennae. The long bobble at the end bounced lightly as he twisted the flexible stem back and forth in his fingers. Diana hated to admit it, but the nervous tick was starting to get rather cute. "Didn't want to risk having to stand around and wait."

"Fair enough."

As Harry had predicted, the restaurant was more or less empty when they arrived, proving the reservation was made more out of nerves than necessity. A few couples were scattered about here or there, but the place had plenty of seating room, and Diana had a hard time seeing this place packed on a weeknight. But the flowers decorating the tables were beautiful, and she imagined the weekends were another matter. Diana and Harry were seated as soon as he mentioned the reservation, and they found themselves in prime real estate next to a rather large glass pane window. The view of the rose garden just outside was downright enchanting, lit by the same hauntingly beautiful blue lights as the greenhouse. Diana spent so much time admiring the flowers, she almost forgot to order when the waitress brought them the bread and water.

Diana didn't fight the smile when she noticed the bread was drenched in butter and tasted like honey.

Or when Harry opened a small packet of honey and dribbled it inside a split open roll.

Dinner was pleasant though the appetizer salads and the start of the main entrees. Diana made a mental note to remember this restaurant for a later date, as this was the best Cobb salad she'd had in ages. The chicken was perfect, with clear grill marks along the side, and the avocado slices were generous. The fried shrimp wrap that Harry had ordered looked pretty amazing, too. Even if the date somehow turned bad in the next hour or so, at the very least, Diana had found a new food spot.

Speaking of her date, Diana watched Harry across the table. He seemed content to eat in the comfortable silence, and didn't press for conversation. The smile on his face was more than enough to hint he was having a good time, and occasionally she'd catch him sneaking peeks in her direction, too. Diana denied her heart skipped a beat when their eyes met.

Maybe he was pretty cute.

"So, um, how long have you dressed like a honey bee?" Diana asked, deciding to learn more about the elephant in the room. She sliced a piece of chicken in half and coated it in the vinaigrette dressing. "It's definitely a unique fashion option."

Diana tried not to wince as she stumbled over that last sentence. There was a fine line between curiosity and outright trying to hurt the guy's feelings. But he was dressed like a honey bee. There had to be something behind that, and Diana felt it was a little important to know if she was going to date the guy.

Harry pulled a piece of shrimp out of his wrap and ate it. He folded the rest of the wrap tighter into a bundle before biting his lip. "It's a little personal."

"I understand. Shouldn't have asked," Diana said. She shoved a piece of chicken in her mouth and inwardly sighed. Harry drooped, and Diana felt like she was walking on eggshells. Had the question been rude? It had been rude. Was he embarrassed? His body language wasn't giving her anything specific to work off of outside of her hurting his feelings somehow, and yet again, the black sclera contacts hid his eyes so there was no help there either. Diana swallowed her food and concentrated on the salad. "It is only the second date."

"Sorry," Harry murmured, lowering his head.

"No," Diana said, pulling her glass over with a grimace. "I shouldn't have asked. Really, it's okay."

"Are you sure?" Harry asked. "I mean, I could——"

"Only if you wanted to, and it doesn't take a detective to tell you don't want to right now," Diana said. She reached over and patted the back of his hand with a smile. "I mean it. So, let's change the subject like good awkward conversationalists."

Harry bit his lip, holding in a laugh, but she saw it in the rise and fall of his chest. Diana felt the the tension from her question slip away, and she relaxed into her seat. Harry cut into his own dish again and Diana was feeling pretty good again.

Hunger satiated, Diana held Harry's arm as they took a last walk around the garden after dinner. The flower exhibits were lovely at night, and once again, Diana added yet another line item to her mental check-list of future things to do during the day. As pretty as everything was in the dark, she had a feeling they were even more impressive in the daylight when all those colors got a chance to really show off. For the most part, Diana controlled where the two of them went as they traveled the well worn paths, Harry content to let her lead.

"I come here a lot," Harry had said, one of his hands slipping into his pocket. The other smoothed the front of his vest. "So I'm okay looking at whatever you want to."

After about ten minutes of aimless wandering, they ended up in a special indoor display dedicated to bonsai trees. Inside the temporary white tent were rows upon rows of small trees ranging in size from one foot to a nearly three foot tall plant that almost looked too big to be a bonsai. Harry followed her around as she looked at each tree, learning all sorts of new things about the miniature plants. Unlike the rest of the garden, this small tent was well lit and everything could be seen in detail.

"They're so cute," Diana said, getting a closer look at an impressive miniature maple. Or at least that's what the little name tag under it said that it was, if she hadn't picked that up from the tiny red, five-sided leaves. "Who knew little tiny trees could be so adorable?"

"Shame they're so much work to maintain, though," Harry said, a table away. His hands were in his pockets and the tips of his antennae touched the leaves as he leaned over for a closer look. The tree he was looking at was one of the larger ones in the exhibit, and had a lovely, twisting shape. "They take a a lot of care."

"Did you read that somewhere, or are you speaking from experience because you tried to raise one?" Diana asked, sneaking in a chance to find more about the odd man.

"The first one. I had thought about getting one once, but I passed when I read up at how much work it was," Harry said, grinning over his shoulder. "I didn't really have time to pay that much attention to only one or two plants."

"So what do you have time for?" Diana pushed a strand of hair behind her ear. She took a few steps closer to Harry's table, and stood shoulder to shoulder with him. She could practically feel the way he tensed, and she hoped it was from the good kind of nerves that made your stomach flutter, and not the terrified kind that made your guts twist. "Like, for fun, I mean?"

"I have a garden," Harry said, taking a single step away so that he could face Diana and see her face. He held his hands up, and made an oval shape with his fingers. "The boss let me have a flower bed in her backyard that I can put anything I want in it. I try to raise a lot of bee friendly flowers, so our yard is always buzzing even though we don't have any hives on the property."

"I bet you love that," Diana said. She hummed, and considered her next question carefully. The night was going so well, that Diana didn't want to risk ruining it, but part of her just had to ask. "Though I am starting to get curious if you do anything that isn't bee related."

Harry stuffed his hands back in his pockets and looked down at the side. He pouted as he mumbled, "I do other stuff."

"Oh?" Diana said, putting her hands behind her back. She walked around him, and leaned over at the waist to look at one of the trees to lighten the stress she was putting on him to answer. "Like what?"

"You'll tease me," Harry muttered.

"Harry, honey, you're dressed like a bee." Diana grabbed one of his antennae and pulled down, tugging his head with it. He gaped at her, eyes wide enough that she caught a sliver of white behind those darned contacts and she laughed, butterflies dancing in her stomach. "You're going to have to work very hard to come up with something weirder than

25

that."

"I'm not weird," Harry said. He pouted harder and turned his head away, but Diana kept their eyes locked by walking around and following his gaze.

Diana tugged on the antennae again, keeping it captive until she got the answer she wanted. Diana teased, "Tell me."

"I have a fairy garden!" Harry blurted.

"A what?" Diana asked, letting go of his antennae. There had been a hundred answers she could have expected from liking romance novels to playing sports of some sort, but Diana hadn't expected that one. She scrunched her nose and asked, "What's a fairy garden?"

Harry straightened his vest, tugging on the end. A dusting of pink was on his cheeks, and he shifted from foot to foot, almost embarrassed. "It's an outdoor craft where you make a small model village. Out of like little houses and stuff. Since it's tiny, it's like you're making a town for fairies. Some people even put little fairy figurines and stuff in it."

"That sounds cute," Diana said, a smile tugging on her lips. He planted flowers for bees and made villages for fairies in his free time. The more she learned about Harry, the more and more she regretted giving up on him that first date. Diana hit her knuckles against the front of Harry's vest a couple times before resting her hand there. "Do you have any pictures? I'd love to see it."

"No," Harry said, looking down where Diana's hand rested on his chest. She could feel his breathing pick up through the fabric, and was half tempted to turn her hand over and see if his heart was beating as loudly as hers was. "I never really thought to take any."

"Can I see it sometime, then?" Diana asked. She swallowed and took a step closer. "I'd love to see what you made."

"Okay," Harry said. He swallowed deeply, and rubbed the ends of his fingers together. Even without seeing his eyes, Diana could tell his mind was racing. "When?"

"How about tonight?" Diana asked, feeling bold. "Or will your hosts get upset to have a visitor around so late?"

"No, it's okay," Harry whispered. "I have my own entrance, so we won't bother them at all."

"Then it's settled," Diana said. She flipped her hand around and patted his chest with her open palm. "The night's still young and we can end the date with a trip to your fairy garden."

Harry nodded stiffly, and followed Diana out of the greenhouse.

Harry's boss lived in a mansion; no wonder her daughter's name was "Princess."

Diana whistled as she stepped out of Harry's car, her feet hitting the cleanly paved drive that ran all the way up to to the side of the home. The house had three floors in addition to what Diana assumed was Harry's attic at the top, and a brilliant balcony wrapped around the entire width of the building on the second and third floors. A small half-balcony was at the top, complete with a staircase that led up the side door that entered the fourth floor attic suite.

In addition to the house, the landscaping itself was a sight to behold. The entire yard was covered in shrubberies and well kept flower beds that likely cost a pretty penny to maintain, unless Harry was doing it for free.

"What a house," Diana said. She tilted her head back as far as it would go, and continued to gape at the stone siding and rich roof tiles.

Harry's joke about working for a bee queen from their first blind date was now officially funnier in hindsight. Diana could definitely see the woman owning this house being as loaded as royalty, and she did work with honey.

"It is pretty nice," Harry said, closing his car door. He walked down the drive and a light blinked on over their heads from the side of the building that caused Diana to jerk to the side when she found herself blinded by a sudden brightness in the dark. Harry shrugged and waved at them. "Motion detectors."

"If she's got that much money, why did she open her shop in an outdoor mall instead of a bigger building?" Diana asked, following Harry to the backyard. As they entered, more lights flickered on from the side of the house, bathing the entire garden in soft, warm light. "Seems like a waste."

"The mall gets more foot traffic, and she had the money before she had the store. Running the honey store is more of a hobby for her than anything," Harry said. He trotted over to the left corner, and stopped next to a small white fence. He waved Diana over and leaned on the edge. "This is my garden."

The garden box was oval in shape and around ten feet long. It was also a good seven feet wide, almost the same size as the two serving bars side by side at the yogurt shop. Diana breathed in the sweet smell of lilac, and brushed her arm against Harry's. The little bed was covered in flowering plants, each one neatly trimmed and kept.

"You put a lot of work into this," Diana said. Leaning over to see some of the flowers in the back, her eye caught something odd. She pointed at a small container filled with smooth stones and water. "What's that?"

"A bee bath," Harry said. He opened the fence and pulled it out so Diana could get a closer look. "The bees can land on the rocks and get a drink of water. You have to refill it every day though, because the water can get dirty or will evaporate since it's so shallow."

"Cute," Diana said. She nudged Harry in the elbow with her own, and grinned. "But I'm pretty sure we're here to see a different sort of garden, aren't we?"

Harry put the bee bath away and pointed in the opposite direction. Diana followed his finger until she spotted a small raised flower bed on the back patio under a lovely wooden pergola. "It's over there."

As they got closer, Diana found the highest point of the flower bed had been raised to waist height. The sides were made of small wood columns that were stacked together like a log cabin house. The top part was covered in rising hills covered in a thick moss, but it was hard to see what else there was in the dark. Harry flipped on the patio lights hanging from the pergola, and Diana put her hands over her mouth and squeaked.

It was adorable.

When Harry had said it was a village, he wasn't kidding. All sorts of tiny houses made out of anything from stumps to twigs, all with tiny windows and doors, were spread out over the fake moss hills. Small welcome mats waited for their "fairy" visitors, and most of the houses had accessories, such as small fruit and vegetable gardens or tiny mail boxes. She saw a small river with water being aided by a pump at the end of the bed from a water wheel, and there was a covered bridge that crossed it. Harry had separated the homes with walking paths and sitting areas with mushroom chairs and tables.

He even had tiny flower pots with small succulent plants filling them spread out everywhere to add some color.

"This is the most adorable thing I have ever seen," Diana said, poking the roof of a cabin-style house built from small sticks and straw. Harry twisted an antennae, staring very hard at a small patio porch on the back of the largest house. Diana tugged on his arm, "How long did it take you to make all of this?"

"Y-you do a little bit a day," Harry said, jerking from Diana's touch. His face flushed and he tugged hard on the antennae. "I've been working on this a little over a year."

"It looks fantastic, Harry," Diana said. She kept her hand on his arm, and rubbed her fingers up and down. "You should be very proud."

"It was fun to make," Harry said, squeezing the top side of the flower bed.

"It's missing something though," Diana said, tapping one of her earrings.

"What?"

"The fairies," Diana said. She squeezed his arm and waved her arm over the bed. "We need to find you some cute little fairies to live in this garden of yours. Be a shame for all these beautiful homes to go to waste."

"May I kiss you?" Harry asked.

The blurted question had come forth so sincere and so shockingly shy that Diana's heart skipped a beat. Harry's shoulders were back, and his lips were slightly parted with his nervous breath. His hands clutched the side of the flower bed, his knuckles turning white with the force of it. His eyes were hidden, but Diana knew they were locked on her face, waiting for an answer. Behind the bee costume and the gardening, was a shy man who wanted to make the most of his second chance.

Diana answered, "Yes."

Harry raised his hands, cupping them around the nape of Diana's neck. His touch was feather light, and the tips of his fingers in her hair sent shivers down her back. She felt his thumbs brush against her jaw as he leaned down, and closed her eyes.

Their lips met.

The warm pressure was inviting and wonderful; sweet like honey and enveloping like a warm blanket.

Diana's hands found their way to Harry's hips, and she pushed up on her tiptoes to deepen the force of the kiss. Harry answered in kind, and the chaste kiss ended with a sweet peck on the lips to finish the moment.

"May I do that again?" Harry whispered, touching their foreheads together.

"Yeah," Diana breathed.

# Chapter 4

"SO, I'M GUESSING someone stepped up to the plate." Jolie whistled, hand on her hip and bubblegum popping. She mimed a bat swing, complete with pointing her finger into the distance after the fake hit. "You look like you scored a home run."

"What did I tell you about equating my love life with baseball?" Diana asked, unwrapping the plastic wrap from the topping containers. She balled the masses of it up and tossed it into the trash can under the counter as each tin was freed from its plastic prison. "I'm pretty sure we talked about that."

"No, you called me a baseball fanatic, and dropped it," Jolie said. She finished putting the till money into the register and asked again. "But for real, you've been smiling all morning. I already know the date went well! So give up the details before the store opens and you try to hide behind customers!"

Diana tossed a ball of plastic wrap at Jolie's head. "Stop that."

"You wouldn't have even said yes if it wasn't for me, so I fully expect details as payment," Jolie said, throwing the projectile right back. Diana attempted to catch it, but it smacked against her fingers and tumbled to the ground. "I'll get the info I want one way or another, so just make it easy on yourself."

"I'll admit you were right," Diana said, picking up the plastic wrap. She shoved it in the container and frowned at her hands. Diana walked to the back to wash them and shouted from the back room. "Giving him another chance was worth it."

"Then tell me everything!" Jolie shouted back. She waved her hands in the air and invaded Diana's personal space. She settled for shaking

Diana's sleeve and grinning as she blew another bubble with her gum. "Did he go dressed as a bee? Where'd he take you? Come on! Don't leave me waiting on third when a single hit'll bring me home!"

"You bring up baseball one more time and I swear I'm not talking to you for the rest of the day," Diana lied. She went back to the task of setting up the toppings bar and rolling her eyes at her desperate friend. Jolie crossed her arms and put on her game face; the one that meant she was going to hit the ball into the scoreboard and win the game no matter what anyone said. Diana caved. "He wore the bee costume, but swapped out the t-shirt for a button up and vest. He took me to that big garden on the outside of town and we had dinner there. It was a lovely night and we both had a very good time."

Jolie squinted her eyes, staring hard at Diana. It felt like the girl was looking through her with newly founded X-ray vision. "There was something else. What was it?"

Diana debated the pros and cons of telling Jolie that she'd invited herself to Harry's home. Knowing Jolie, she'd jump straight to conclusions, but that wasn't the real issue. Diana wasn't sure yet if it was her place to tell anyone that Harry had a fairy garden. He seemed so self conscious about it, and Diana didn't want to ruin the first good start to a relationship by destroying his trust.

Fate intervened in the form of knocking on the yogurt store glass.

Jolie popped another bubble, and Diana blinked at the young girl banging her fist on the door. Princess practically shoved her face against the glass, demanding attention a good hour before store open. The anger on her face promised murder, and Diana considered leaving her out there.

Expectedly, Jolie opened the door for her.

"You!" Princess shouted, shoving past Jolie and into the main floor of the shop. She rounded the serving bar and stopped an inch from Diana. "What'd you do to him?"

"What are you talking about?" Diana asked. There was only one "him" that Princess could be referring to, and last Diana checked he was fine! "Did something happen to Harry?"

Princess squawked, her mouth hanging open like a fish. "And now you're calling him that?"

"Did something happen to Harry or not?" Diana repeated. She squared her shoulders, standing as tall as possible to hold her ground.

"You came all the way over here to bang on my door, and I'm really hoping there's a reason for it."

"He's a mess!" Princess said, throwing her hands up. She put her hands on her hips and made a show of sticking her nose in the air. "He can't concentrate, he keeps humming, and his head is stuck in the clouds. He even forgot to bring his lunch today!"

"Sounds like he had a good time at their date last night, too," Jolie said, poking her finger into the side of Princess' head. With the height difference, Jolie had to stand on her tip-toes to do it, and Diana had to bite her lip to stop from laughing. Jolie popped another bubble, grinning and chewing as obnoxiously loud as she could. "You should be happy you've got a lovestruck bee on your hands."

"That's not the point!" Princess shouted, pointing at Diana. The fire continued to burn in her eyes and Diana wondered for the first time if she'd have competition for Harry. Princess fumed, her face contorting with her rage. "First she stands him up, and now she's got him all weird. She's trouble and should stay away."

Diana asked, "How old are you, Princess?"

"Wh-what's that got to do with anything?" Princess asked, huffing.

"You're acting like a child, that's what," Diana returned. She went back to her toppings bar, making sure that the plastic wrap was removed. The store opened soon and she didn't have time for this. "Harry's a grown man, and he can make his own decisions."

"Yeah, but he doesn't always look out for himself, so someone's got to," Princess said, pressing her lips together as she finished. Her cheeks burned with red, surely a mix of anger and embarrassment at this point. "So if he doesn't get his act together, it's your fault."

With that, Princess turned on her heel and stormed out of the yogurt shop as quickly as she had come in. Diana could almost see the steam coming from her ears, complimenting the red anger on her face.

"And here I thought in-laws were usually the worst you had to deal with when dating someone," Jolie said, laughing and shoving Diana lightly in the shoulder. "That girl's going to be a handful. What a coworker."

"He lives in the apartment above her house," Diana admitted, shaking her head. "So she practically is an in-law."

"Ouch," Jolie laughed. She leaned on Diana's shoulder, taking her elbow and holding onto it. She whispered, "Is he worth it?"

"So far," Diana said, tilting her head against Jolie's. "I think so."

On a whim, a week after Princess had invaded the yogurt shop, Diana decided to drop by the honey store on her long journey back to the parking garage. She wasn't sure of the store's hours, and there was a chance she'd either catch it just as it was closing, or just after everything was already locked up. Despite all the time that had passed, Diana had yet to actually go inside Harry's store.

She supposed it couldn't hurt to see some of the things that he liked. Diana was learning about bees in order to get to know a potential boyfriend better. Who would have thought?

The honey store was still open when she arrived, and Diana hiked her tote bag higher on her shoulder. She tugged her work cap off her head and shoved it in the bag as she entered. Diana reached up and tugged out her ponytail, fixing her hair discretely via her front store window reflection.

Harry's store was about the same size as the yogurt shop, with the same layout as the rest of the stores on the strip. Which meant that the door off to the back led to the employee area, and there should be a restroom at the very back of the store. The rest of the place was laid out quite differently, of course. Instead of a wall of yogurt machines on the back wall, and a toppings bar, there were book shelves and tables covered in jars of honey. All of them were neatly labeled, and the jar types varied from every shape type from the standard bear-bottle to large mason jars.

She smiled at the ones that had huge chunks of honey comb floating in them, and picked up a small one that had a cute picture on the label. Diana figured she might as well buy something while she was here. It's not like she hated honey. She just preferred it in smaller doses.

Carrying the palm-sized jar, Diana wandered toward the back and noticed a fake wall set up to divide a small corner from the rest of the store. She stuck her head inside the opening, and found large, stacked boxes with pictures of bee cases, and all sorts of other equipment against the walls and shelves. Harry had said there was bee keeping equipment for people who wanted it. How-to books lined the far wall on a shelf, and it looked like there was a decent selection.

Not interested in that half of the business, Diana stepped out and went to look at the back wall shelves. Now that she had a closer look, she found there was only honey on the middle shelves. The labels weren't in English, so Diana took a guess that this was the import section. The bottom shelves had random bee-related knick-knacks on them, and the top shelves had toys and cute stuffed plushes.

This place had anything and everything you could have wanted that was bee or honey related, but there was still something missing: An employee.

Diana wasn't sure if she'd see Harry or not, because she had yet to ask for his schedule, but there had to be someone watching the shop right? As much as she wanted to avoid it, Diana was even prepared for another meeting with Princess.

Holding her jar of honey, Diana wandered up to the check out counter and called out, "Hello?"

The staff room door popped open, and Harry's head came into view. He saw Diana and his face lit up into a smile so bright it almost made Diana blush on the spot. She couldn't think of anyone else who was that happy to see her every time they saw her. Harry stumbled out of the back room and came to the counter. He licked his lips and said, "Hey."

"Should you be hiding in the back room when the store's still open?" Diana teased, putting her jar of honey on the counter. "What if I'd been another customer?"

"I was organizing some stock to bring out," Harry admitted. He laughed and rested his hands on the counter. "The store's usually dead around this time, so it's pretty safe to leave the front unattended for ten or twelve minutes."

"You're here alone?"

"No," Harry said, shaking his head. "Princess is just on break. She'll be back in twenty minutes to help close."

"That's good. Hate for you to be working the whole store by yourself," Diana said. She would have gone crazy if she had to attend a dead store with nothing to do and no one to talk to all day. Even Jolie's baseball puns were better than nothing.

"What brings you by?" Harry asked. He pulled down his sleeves, his fingers bunching in the material in a cute, nervous gesture. "Looking for honey?"

"I wanted to see where you worked," Diana said. She waved behind her and shrugged. "You've been to the yogurt shop a few times now, and I've yet to see yours from closer than the front windows."

"Like it?"

"Yeah, it's nice," Diana said. She pushed her jar forward and shrugged. "And I figured I might as well get a jar of honey while I'm here."

Harry nodded and picked up her selection. He flipped the label over and grinned. "Good choice. Marty makes some of the best clover honey we've got in the store."

"I'll take your word for it," Diana said. "Most honey I buy is from the supermarket, so I'm sure pretty much anything in here is probably better."

"By miles," Harry laughed. He rang up her purchase, with his hand still on the jar. "I know I'm biased, but local honey is always better than the processed stuff. And your total is $1.26."

Diana handed him the money without complaint, surprised the price was so low. She had expected it to cost a little more for the convince of local bought.

"It's a small jar," Harry said, as if reading her mind. "And the guy who makes it lives down the street from my boss. He doesn't have to add in transport costs to his price, and just drops the stuff off for me to carry in. Means he can charge less here."

"That's convenient," Diana said. "Guess I really did pick a good one."

"And hopefully you can come back and try some others," Harry offered, handing her the honey jar wrapped in a small bag. "If you wanted."

"I think I'd like that," Diana said, taking the bag. Harry smiled, and she found herself warming and a smile of her own growing on her face. "You'll have to show me the good ones."

Harry grinned, resting his arms on the counter. His antennae bounced from the motion, and he shifted his wings behind him. "I'd love to."

It looked like her honey wasn't the only good choice she'd made lately.

# CHAPTER 5

THIS TIME, DIANA asked Harry out.

It felt like the best course of action, especially since Harry had gone bashful after their first date. He visited Diana quite a bit at the yogurt shop still, and Diana waved as she passed his honey shop on the way to and from work, but they hadn't had another big date. No garden trips. No hints at another meal together. Nothing. Not a thing had come up to take them from "friends who had a single date" to "dating."

And Diana didn't appreciate that.

She touched her lips as she stared in the mirror, looking over her latest outfit before she left. If she closed her eyes, she could still feel the last time they kissed in that garden under the pergola. Diana was in the mood for another one of those if she could get it, and since Harry wasn't going to make a move in public (and Diana wasn't still sure if they were a proper item or not), that meant another date was in order. Since Harry hadn't asked yet, it was up to Diana.

So she'd asked, they were going out, and surely that would lead to another goodnight kiss.

Logic at its finest.

She looked at the clock out of the corner of her eye as she straightened her vest. She had another ten minutes before she had to leave to pick up Harry if she didn't want to be late. Putting her hopes for the night aside, Diana completed one last mirror check to make sure she still looked great.

Harry wasn't the only one who was meticulous about what to wear.

Her khaki slacks hung well off her legs, and did little to distract from the flower-print of her long-sleeved shirt. Diana smirked, amused that for both dates she'd worn some sort of flower ensemble for her bee-dressed companion. They were going to be a regular matching set at this rate. She straightened the black vest she'd chosen and made sure her collar was buttoned before she picked up a small fairy broach to clip to the fabric. She'd dug the thing out of her closet last week when she'd remembered it was back there. It had been a gift from her mother or something. She couldn't remember.

But it felt appropriate to wear all the same.

More than ready to go, Diana grabbed her keys and purse, skipping out her front door with a smile. The afternoon sun was still out and the evening sky had Diana in a good mood as she trotted down to her car. Her little four-door wasn't as nice as Harry's, but it would get them where they needed to go.

Diana had to contain the butterflies in her stomach the entire drive out to Harry's place, concentrating on both the radio and paying attention to directions. The last thing she needed was to get lost driving out to the middle of nowhere. But, thankfully, she made it there with time to spare.

Harry waited for her, sitting on the bottom few steps of the outdoor stairs that led to his attic home. He had on a mix of his usual daily ensemble with what he wore on their garden date which gave him a cute dressed up, but still casual, sort of look. The black jeans with painted-on yellow stripes looked good on him, and Diana liked his button up yellow shirt. The best part: He'd finished it all off with his black vest.

Diana looked down at her own vest and snorted. Matching set, indeed!

"Hope you weren't waiting long," Diana said, hopping out of her car almost as soon as she'd finished parking it. She twirled her keys on her hand as she trotted up to the steps, her gaze following Harry as he stood. "Traffic was a little heavier than I was expecting."

"No, didn't wait long," Harry said. He pointed up to a small window on the attic level. "Didn't even head downstairs until I saw your headlights in the distance from the comfort of my room."

Diana turned, looking down the long baron road that led up to the house. "You made it down four flights of steps with enough time to sit and wait in the four minutes it took me to come down that drive?"

"It was ten minutes to get down the drive," Harry said, putting his hands in his pockets. He passed her, his feet tapping lightly on the drive. Harry smirked over his shoulder, amused and happy. "And it only takes me two to get down the stairs."

Diana stuck her tongue out at him and turned back toward her car. "Get in. I didn't make a reservation, so we might want to get a move on before their rush hits."

"Yes ma'am," Harry said.

For dinner, Diana had chosen her favorite Greek restaurant.

It was part of a chain, but her grandmother had gone to the first mom and pop place that had started it when she was a teenager, and swore by it to this day. She said she knew the owner, and that the man was very strict with the quality of food that went into the rest of the locations. Diana'd been taken to them all over the country during family visits and vacations (it was a requirement to eat there at least once whenever two people in her family got together for any reason), and she knew the food was pretty standard across the board. And of course, when your Greek grandmother tells you the food's authentic, you tend to take her word for it.

Though Diana ate there less for authenticity, and more because they served the best lamb and rice she'd ever had, save for the one time she'd actually been to visit Greece. It really didn't get much better than that, and having her family's stamp of approval only made it better. This restaurant was good food and good memories all wrapped into one.

When Diana had told Jolie where she was taking Harry, her friend had grinned and said, "So, you're like practicing to introduce him to the family? That's so cute!"

She hadn't really thought of it that way, but it was sort of true. Diana associated this restaurant with family, and now she was inviting Harry into that place. But then again, getting more serious with Harry about their relationship was part of the point. So, to Greek food it was!

Diana pulled into the parking lot on, and unbuckled. Harry rubbed his thumb against his other hand, drawing a small circle. It was a different sort of nervous twitch than his bashful playing with his antennae and Diana paused. "You okay?"

"Yeah, I'm fine," Harry said. He breathed in and out slowly. Diana could practically see him counting to ten in his head, and her stomach began to twist in unexpected nerves. Harry mumbled, "Just haven't been out to a new place in a while."

"Used to routine?" Diana asked, getting out. She waited for Harry to do the same before finishing, resting her elbows on the top of her car. "I can respect that. Not everyone likes adventure."

"Adventure I can handle," Harry said. He looked at the restaurant and shook his head, the fluff around his neck ruffling in the wind. "It's people that scare me."

"Don't worry," Diana said. She rounded the car and took his arm. She squeezed it before dropping her hand down his sleeve and grabbing his hand, lacing their fingers together. "The food will make you forget all about them and let you be your delightful, introverted self."

"Will it now?" Harry asked.

"Or at least the dessert will," Diana said, raising her eyebrow. "Authentic baklava made with local honey."

Harry blushed, laughing into his other hand. "Okay, you've got me."

"Knew that was your ticket."

Diana held his hand the entire way into the restaurant, her heart quick and adrenaline picking up. This was going to be a great night. Her favorite restaurant, and a guy who was quickly becoming one of her favorite fellas. What a wonderful combination.

Diana hadn't factored in the whispering when she had made plans.

She rested her chin in her hands, finding it hard to meet Harry's gaze when his eyes were laser focused on the table and the menu in his hands. The strange look the hostess had given them when they walked in was the first clue, but it wasn't until they were walking through the restaurant and they received the mixture of giggles and hushed whispers that she realized everyone was staring at her and Harry.

Specifically, Harry's bee costume.

Diana sipped her soda, wondering if it was appropriate she was more embarrassed than Harry was at the moment. No wonder he was nervous when they got out of the car. "Haven't been to a new place in a while" and "it's the people that scare me" didn't have anything to do with Harry being shy. So far, they'd met at that tiny mom and pop cafe, the mall, the garden, and it just hit Diana that those were all places where people were familiar with Harry. Where people wouldn't stare. Diana was mortified she had forgotten that people would make fun of Harry in a new place.

Even Diana had done it when they first met.

"This is a nice place," Harry said, eyes on the menu and a small tremor in his hand. It was a nice place. Diana looked at the Greek vase in the wall indent at the end of the table, and the geometric patterns on the table. The decor and warm atmosphere weren't as pleasant as they usually were with teenagers snickering at you two tables away. Harry was a trooper doing his best to ignore them. "What's good?"

"Everything, honestly," Diana said. She forced a smile and decided to focus on the food. The food was amazing and delicious, and the staff were nice. They'd get through this focusing on the highlights of the evening and have something fond to remember. Diana reached across the table and flipped a menu page over. She pointed at a small section at the bottom. "But I'd recommend starting with a gyro if you want to play it safe. You've got your choice of beef, chicken or lamb."

"That sounds good," Harry said. He dared to look up, keeping his attention on Diana instead of the room. She smiled at him brightly as she could, and his shoulders relaxed. Good. It was just the two of them here. Diana, Harry and good food. That's exactly what they needed to focus on. "I think I'll get the——"

A rolled napkin cut Harry off. It had hit the side of his cheek hard enough that he flinched.

Diana swung her head over to the table full of teenagers and they laughed. One of them had the audacity to claim they were throwing it at themselves and missed. She knew better. Harry hunched forward, hiding his height as he tried to make himself smaller. He knew better. Diana felt like someone had reached into her chest and yanked her heart out, seeing his broken expression.

"Which one did you want?" Diana asked, turning in her seat to flag down the waiter. "Filling wise."

"Lamb?" Harry said, voicing his answer as a question as he tried to figure out what Diana was doing. "Figured I'd try something new. Is something wrong?"

"Yup," Diana said. When the waiter finally came back to their table (Diana had been so distracted by the staring, she hadn't noticed her waiter had taken longer than normal to help them), she spared no time speaking her mind. "You know, we've changed our minds. We're going to have our order to go. I want two gyros, both lamb, and an order of baklava. We'll wait for it at the front and pay there."

Diana picked up her purse and grabbed Harry's hand before he could say anything. He stayed quiet as she marched him straight to the front and sat them both down in the waiting area. Anyone who dared to look at them funny received the worst glare Diana could send them. She crossed her arms over her chest and mentally mapped out the area for some place close they could eat where they could be alone that wasn't one of their houses. This was supposed to be a night out, not a night in. There was a park a few blocks down that might work, though it was a bit late and getting dark out.

"Sorry," Harry said, interrupting her thoughts.

"What are you sorry for?" Diana asked, turning her head. "You didn't do anything wrong."

"You were really excited about eating here," Harry said, shifting in his seat and adjusting his wings behind him. They curled around the bench seat toward the front. "And now we're leaving because I'm drawing too much attention. Because of the—"

"It's my fault," Diana said before he could insult himself. She looked at Harry and pressed her lips together. She sucked in a breath and leaned against his arm. "I've gotten so used to it, I had completely forgotten that your outfit was weird to other people. It didn't even cross my mind you would get teased."

She watched the floor, and Harry stayed quiet, but she could feel the way he trembled.

"I'm the one who's sorry." Diana hadn't meant to hurt him. She really hadn't. Diana laced their arms together and held it tight. "I'm sorry I put you in a position to be teased when we were supposed to be having a good night."

Harry still didn't respond, and Diana couldn't help but wonder what he had been thinking. She had barely said his name to get his attention when she looked up, and saw the warmest smile on his face she'd seen yet. Not a joyful expression, nor a bitter one. It was content and warm; a small, welcome lift of his lips.

"Are you okay?" Diana asked. Her lip quirked and she patted his hand. "You look pretty happy for someone who was assaulted with a napkin earlier."

"I'm just really happy right now," Harry said. He leaned over and kissed the top of Diana's head. His face hovered there for a second before he nuzzled his face into her hair, cuddling on the waiting bench. His gravely voice whispered into her hair, sending shivers down her spine. "It's been a long time since someone forgot my clothes were weird."

"Oh," Diana breathed. She shifted, tucking herself under his arm and into his side. She leaned her head on his shoulder and hummed. "I'm glad then."

The rest of the night went by too fast. They got their food, and ate it in the park, both happy they'd picked the gyro when they found themselves needing the pita bread wrap to hold the food together as they sat on the hood of her car eating in the well lit parking lot. Diana remembered laughing with him, and how sweet the baklava tasted when Harry split his dessert with her.

They shared the fork.

But more importantly, she remembered how long his lips lingered on hers when she dropped him off at home, and how she almost followed him up the stairs to his room after he said goodnight.

# CHAPTER 6

DIANA OPENED THE door to the garden shop, and whistled at the sheer size of it. The warehouse building went on for what seemed like miles, filled with shelves covered in plants and tools, all neatly kept under high bay lights. Diana couldn't see the back wall from where she was standing, and got the feeling that this building would dwarf most department stores if she had to compare in size. But if any shop was going to have what she needed, this was it. Diana shoved the list of directions in her back pocket, and headed into the busy metroplex of flowers.

It'd been about two weeks since their not-a-complete-disaster date at the Greek restaurant, and Diana could confidently say that she and Harry were now an item.

They'd been out together a few times since then, furthering this idea, though Diana had let Harry pick the dating locations to be safe. She had no intention of making the same mistake twice and putting that man through all that public teasing again. Most of their dates turned out pretty okay, and were either garden trips or locations at the mall where everyone seemed to know him already. The most memorable of which, however, was probably their trip to the art gallery. It was both someplace new, but also empty enough of other guests that it was easy to avoid any cruel and mocking glances that came their way.

But even that trip ended a bit short, not that it wasn't for the better.

The art gallery had had an exhibit on honeycomb sculptures, which were interesting to say the least. Apparently you could make bees create different shapes with their honeycomb if you had the right molds, and the little gallery had every shape from diamonds to sculptures of people's heads. Diana couldn't say she cared for them, and funny enough, Harry found them rather boring as well. They both had a wonderful laugh about it, and Diana ended the date with a cute little bee pin Harry bought for her in the gift shop. Well, that and a wonderful kiss goodnight on the doorstep of her house when he dropped her off at home.

That particular kiss lasted quite a bit longer than their previous ones, and Diana could still feel Harry's fingers digging into her skin.

Diana distracted herself from her daydreams and picked up a small pamphlet on the side aisle of the store. She opened it up and held it in front of her face to hide the blush as she thought about Harry's hands on her waist, and their hips pressed together. Diana shook her head. *Read the pamphlet,* she commanded herself. She didn't have time to get distracted. She was on a mission!

Taking a good look at the glossy paper in her hands, Diana frowned. It was a map. This place was so large it needed a map to get around. She folded the brochure back up and continued wandering the aisles. She wasn't completely sure what she wanted to get him, but it was nice she had a map.

If she'd learned anything about Harry on their subsequent dates after the restaurant, it was at the garden. Harry was a regular customer there, so it was one of the few places where no one gave him a second look for dressing like himself, and the exhibits were so large you could hardly see it all in one trip anyway. Harry was more knowledgeable about flowers than Diana had originally realized, and as he relaxed around Diana, the flower facts came open and freely as they passed each exhibit. He even held her hand as he dragged her around and both times had been so casual and pleasant that Diana already found herself looking forward to the next date and the next and the next.

She felt warm and fuzzy around Harry in a way that she hadn't expected, and it made her want to do something for him. Somehow going out wasn't enough, and Diana really wanted to get him a present. A good one. Not just a jar of honey he could get every day, or a new flower for his garden. Diana wanted to make sure it was something really special to let him know that next steps for their relationship might be in order in the near future.

A couple of kids dashed by her from the aisle just to her left, laughing and screaming as they waved garden tools at each other like swords. Diana relaxed her shoulders and laughed, before taking in a shaky breath and looking out over the aisles upon aisles of potential presents.

If she couldn't find a perfect present for Harry in here, considering how much he loved flowers and gardening, she wasn't sure what she'd do. The guy already had the bee angle covered, and Diana wanted to prove she saw more of him than just the bees and honey he paraded around. The point was to show that she listened to him; that she noticed he did have other interests!

It had to be something for his fairy garden.

Diana turned the corner, dodging around a large stand full of pots and odd shaped jars that were stacked in the center, and looked up at the signs. The map Diana had burned in her pocket, but she just knew that she'd stumble upon the perfect gift if she wandered at random. Call it gut instinct or stubbornness, but that's what it was. Jolie would be proud Diana was sticking to her guns of "I'll know the gift when I see it."

Instead, Diana saw fountains, yard care supplies, and all sorts of other things, but none of them seemed to be what her gut was looking for.

At the fifth aisle toward the back, Diana stopped at a small hardware section. She walked inside and found herself surrounded by small houses made of stumps and other pieces of wood. Tiny furniture. Diana crossed her arms and smiled at all the adorable creations, pre-made to start off someone's fairy garden. Harry hadn't been kidding; it might have been a more popular hobby than Diana first thought.

But these gardens were missing the same thing that Harry's was.

At the first sign of a colored vest, Diana flagged down the store worker and asked for directions. She had no time to waste looking now that she knew exactly what she wanted. The employee confirmed Diana could find what she came for and she nearly giggled in delight as she sprinted down the aisle toward the proper section.

Harry was going to love it.

She watched Harry set up a display of honey jars through the window. Diana checked her watch, knowing that he went on lunch break in about ten minutes. Princess was behind the counter, and wanting to avoid a confrontation was the only reason Diana hadn't already invited herself into the store to see Harry. She had his gift wrapped nice and neat in a bag in her hand, and she took a step outside of the window to stand on the wall and wait.

Diana checked her watch, wondering if it was too presumptuous to show up on his lunch break. She huffed and held the gift bag behind her back. She could have waited until after the little honey store closed, but she had already promised Jolie they'd hang out at her place after work, and she wanted to give Harry the gift today. Diana rubbed the back of her neck, her other hand holding tight to the bag. The rough string handle dug into her skin with how hard she squeezed.

She hoped he liked it.

Harry appeared through the door yawning into his hand. He rubbed his arm through his dark sleeves and the sleepy look on his face was rather adorable, even with the pitch black eyes. Diana grinned, happy she had gone unnoticed as he walked by. Lunch was definitely the right time to catch him off guard.

Diana snuck behind him and reached up above his wings to tug on the furry collar around his throat. "Got you!"

He jerked and turned around, but the angry look melted away the second he saw Diana, and realized it was friendly teasing. "Diana."

"Hey," Diana said, pushing her hair behind her ear. He smiled, and she smiled right back. Diana prayed his immediate reaction to her presence never went away; it was addictive. "I had the day off and thought I'd surprise you for lunch."

"That'd be great," Harry said. He pointed down the street toward the open food court and the sheepish smile on his face made Diana want to reach up and pinch his cheek. "Though I've only got time to catch something quick at the mall."

"That's fine," Diana said. She hooked her arm through his and tugged him along. If they only had a little bit of time, they might as well get moving while they good. "I know how fast lunch breaks can go!"

"What's in the bag?" Harry asked, looking down at her hand.

His eyes had locked immediately to the yellow and black wrapping paper and Diana winked at him. "That's a surprise."

Harry huffed, but it was the amused sort with a twitching smile on his face, so Diana let him huff and puff all he wanted. She sat him down at a table and asked what he wanted, refusing to let Harry argue about paying. Diana put her hands on her hips and put the bag on the table. "I'm treating today, so what do you want?"

"I like the number two combo at the Chinese place," Harry said, glancing at the defenseless gift bag. He put his hands on the table and laced his fingers together, fidgeting. "If you don't mind."

"You've got it," Diana said. She ruffled Harry's hair as he sat down, careful not to knock his antennae off, and grinned at the embarrassed face he made. All her nervousness from earlier melted away simply from being around him. She stopped when she felt good and truly relaxed, her fingers lingering in the blond hair. She smoothed it back down into place and placed a quick kiss on his forehead. "I'll be right back, and don't you dare look in that bag!"

"I won't," Harry said, shoving his hands on his thighs to keep from touching.

Satisfied that he wasn't going to sneak a peek, Diana headed to the Chinese food section of the food court and waited in line. Looking over her shoulder, she caught Harry poking the side of the gift bag, but was making no move to tip it over and venture behind the crackling tissue paper barrier. She covered her mouth to hide the grin, and hoped the line would move faster. Soon enough, her turn came and Diana headed back to the table with a tray of two plates of lo mein and two sodas.

Diana sat the drink and plate in front of Harry as she sat down, helping herself to the seat on his left at the small square table. "I see you restrained yourself."

"It was difficult," Harry admitted, turning behind him to pull his wings closer to himself as people passed behind. Sitting, the tips of them dragged on the ground and Diana wondered how many people had stepped on them before in the busy food court. Harry cut into his food, talking around bites of thick noodles. "Makes me wonder if I forgot an occasion."

"No occasion," Diana said. She fiddled with her drink before digging into the food. She scooped up a mouthful of fried rice and nudged him with the tip of her finger. "Saw it in a store and thought it was perfect for you."

Or it better be perfect after Diana had wandered around for two hours in a garden store this morning looking for the perfect present.

Harry tugged the bag over by the side and tipped it to the side, just enough to tease a look, but not actually see the gift through the mountain of tissue paper Diana had wrapped it in. "Can I open it now, or do I have to wait?"

"Now or later," Diana said, shrugging. She crossed her fingers in her head for now, but thought it best to give him the option. Though she was pretty sure he'd cave and open it now. So much of Harry's personality was excitable like a child, that she bet he loved opening presents as soon as possible. "Up to you."

Harry pushed away his empty plate and tugged on the tissue paper. It crinkled and soon joined a tiny ripped pile on the side of the table. He dug into the bag, pulling out the first of six small wrapped packages in the bottom. He held it in his hand and glanced at Diana. "There's more than one thing in here."

"They're part of a set," she said, crossing one leg over the other. She placed her empty plates on top of his and stacked their trays. She pushed them to the side to give him more room to unwrap the gifts. Diana rested her chin on her hands. "Couldn't just get one."

Harry tugged open the wrapping paper on the first one, and gaped. Diana felt her heart stop as his mouth hung open and he held the tiny present, stock still. She waited, and he kept staring at the gift like he couldn't believe it was in his hands. Was this a good sign or a bad one? Diana forced her breathing to stay even as she waited for his response.

She hadn't guessed wrong had she?

He gently traced his finger along the glittering wing on the small fairy figurine and looked straight at Diana. His voice was a whisper, "It's a fairy."

"I told you," Diana said, biting the edge of her pinky finger as she hunched her shoulders. "Your garden looked lonely."

The fairy figurine had a dress made of yellow daffodils. She had large butterfly wings made of sparkling blue, and Diana had been assured that she was weather-proof enough to keep her paint outside. Her flower hat, made of smaller daffodils in a bunch, was particularly cute. The little fairy was about half the size of Harry's palm, and he held the figurine like it was something precious.

He looked in the rest of the bag, and his voice raised in excitement. "Are they all fairies?"

"Well, four more fairies and one rather large dragonfly that had a saddle and set of reins I thought was cute," Diana said, her voice rushed from nerves. As his face continued to turn up in the sweet smile Diana had come to love, she calmed, every inch of her relaxing in relief. She'd guessed right. This had been perfect, but she had to check. Had to make sure: "Do you like them?"

"I love them," Harry said, his voice full and almost wet with gratitude.

He rewrapped the little daffodil fairy and put her back in the bag with the others. He pulled the bag over and practically hugged it against his chest. "I can't wait to get home and open the rest. I'd do it now, but lunch is over and I don't want to break any of them."

"I'm really glad you like them," Diana said, amused at how his voice had quickened.

"I really, really do," Harry said, squeezing the bag with one arm. He leaned over and kissed Diana on the cheek, while his other hand found the back of her neck and tugged the two of them closer. His fingertips lingered on her skin as he whispered, "I'll see you later."

Harry ran off, leaving her alone with a pounding heartbeat and no breath. Diana rubbed the spot on his cheek where he'd kissed her.

# CHAPTER 7

"YOU'VE GOT IT so bad," Jolie said, leaning over Diana's shoulder to grab her cup. She slurped down a gulp of soda and smacked the drink down on the table in front of them. Diana didn't look at her, but she was positive Jolie was grinning so widely her face might split in two any second. "Just look at you blushing talking about him!"

"I'm not blushing," Diana said, slumping down into the beanbag chair. She munched on a mouthful of popcorn out of the baseball painted plastic bowl. Diana spoke through her chewing, not caring it was rude. It was only Jolie. "You're blushing."

"You bet I am!" Jolie squeaked, falling back into her couch. Diana rattled the last few kernels of popcorn around int he bowl before putting it on the table. Crossing her arms, she sunk into the beanbag hoping to disappear. Jolie stuck her feet up on the coffee table, rattling their drinks and twisted back and forth on the couch. "It's just so cute! How could I not?"

"Glad you're enjoying yourself," Diana huffed. She stretched her legs out under the table, and crossed them at the ankles. She leaned her head on the couch cushion, her hair a few inches from Jolie's side. "So what about you? Ever ask out that batter?"

"Not yet, or rather, I won't be getting to it at all," Jolie said, humming and fixing up her air in a messy bun. She rolled full on her back and sighed at the ceiling. Her legs slipped off the table, knocking Diana in the side. Jolie tugged them up to the couch a second later, getting them out of the way. "I was going to, but then I found out he's got a girl and decided it might not be the best to ask out a guy who's been going steady with the same lady for two years."

"Rough." Diana passed over the bowl of popcorn, rolling on her side and digging into the bean bag chair. She reached up and patted Jolie on the leg as comfortingly as possible. "At least you found out before you embarrassed yourself or something."

"Something like that," Jolie leaned over, a calculating look on her face that spelled all sorts of trouble. She wasn't paying any attention to the baseball game on the television, and that worried Diana more than it should have. A focused Jolie was a dangerous Jolie. She shoved Diana in the shoulder and hummed. "But it really isn't about me, is it? Right now things are about you."

"And what's there to know about me?" Diana asked, cursing that her redirection to change the subject to Jolie's love life had failed. One of these days they'd talk about Jolie's love life and keep the topic on Jolie's love life. Diana pulled down her soda and chewed the straw. "Dating's going well, and since you usually find out the nitty gritty details anyway, I don't think there's a problem that needs so much attention."

"You're missing my point. I mean, how serious are you going to take things?" Jolie asked, biting the edge of her lip. She tugged on the back of Diana's hair, turning on her side. "I mean, are you going to take it to the next level and see if he wears that bee costume in bed, or what?"

"Jolie!" Diana said, turning around and shoving a pillow from the floor in her friend's face. Jolie let go of the bowl and it clattered to the ground. Kernels spilled on the floor, but neither moved to get them. Diana pressed the pillow harder into Jolie's face so she couldn't see Diana's red one. "What sort of question is that?"

"A legitimate one!" Jolie laughed, fending off the pillow with the skills of a champ. All that athletic practice worked in her favor and Diana cursed when the pillow was snatched away with little effort. Jolie hugged it to her chest and pulled her legs up to sit crossed legged on the couch. She grinned, the scandalous smile and narrowed eyes showed off the lewd places her mind had already gone. "You've been dating for a while now. Why not invite yourself over?"

"I'm not talking about this with you," Diana said. She turned away from Jolie and crossed her arms as she sank into the beanbag chair. "At all."

But Jolie's damage had been done and the thoughts were in Diana's head before she could stop them. Her cheeks heated from the thought of Harry with his shirt off, and the hint of his hips from the lowered waist line of unbuttoned jeans. Worst of all, Diana found she couldn't picture him without the furry collar, the wings, or the antennae on his head no matter how hard she tried, and that made her cheeks blush all the harder. That costume had become so much of a part of him, she wondered if he really did take the thing off at night.

Or if she'd even want him, too.

Diana groaned covering her face as a flash of needy, black eyes stared at her from her own mind. She rolled over, shoving her cheek into the side of the beanbag chair and dug her fingers into the side. "I've got it so bad."

"You do," Jolie said, patting the top of Diana's head.

The next morning at work, Diana yet again regretted telling Jolie anything about her love life.

"I set the fairies up in the garden," Harry said, digging a spoon into his cup of yogurt. Diana watched him from behind the toppings counter, smiling as she wiped the surface down. It was Harry's turn to have a day off, and he celebrated it with yogurt and keeping Diana company. A few customers were huddled on the other side of the room, but it was quiet enough they could chat without issue. "You were right. The place looks much better with some residents."

"You should invite her over to see it in person," Jolie spoke up from the register. She popped a bubble from her gum and winked as obnoxiously as possible. The confirmation of just how badly Diana wanted to see Harry with his shirt off had turned Jolie ruthless. That girl had gone on the attack, and dropped any hint of being subtle. "You two haven't been back to your place since then right? I bet she'd love to see it in the daytime."

Harry stopped with his spoon halfway to his mouth, and slowly finished the bite with a thoughtful look on his face. He reached up and tugged on the end of his antennae, running the fuzzy end back and forth between his fingers. "I wouldn't mind if you came over again."

"And maybe this time you can actually show her your place," Jolie said, unhelpfully. Diana nearly threw something at her to get her to shut up, but there were other customers in the store. She couldn't cause a scene. Jolie grinned, knowing she had momentary immunity. "I heard last time, she only got to see the backyard."

"It was late and I had to bring her home," Harry said, fidgeting with his spoon. He dug around in the yogurt, burying a cherry under the frozen dessert. He mumbled, "And I didn't have time to clean up beforehand."

"Diana wouldn't have minded," Jolie said, grinning. "My place is always a wreck and she doesn't care."

"Diana is right here," Diana said. It was not a big deal they'd been going out this long and hadn't been back to Harry's place for anything longer than getting in the car and leaving. They liked going out for dates. There was no reason for Jolie to tease them! In retaliation, and to get her friend to shut up, Diana threw a napkin at Jolie's head, pretending to aim for the trashcan. It smacked into Jolie's temple and she said, "Oops, missed the bin."

"Yeah, missed all right," Jolie said. She put the paper in the bin for her and grinned at Harry. "But for real, Diana would love to see your room. She's been—"

"Jolie!" Diana said, shoving the girl in the side, a hiss of warning in her voice. "Stop teasing him."

Harry had turned bright red at the table, and had taken to focusing very hard on his yogurt. She wondered what he was thinking, and the second Diana had a hint of what put that blush on his face, had one spreading on her own. Diana turned away from the laughing Jolie and rubbed her cheeks, willing the color to go away. Perhaps if she chased away the blush, the thoughts of Harry with ruffled hair and no shirt would run away, too.

Or she could focus on the real deal sitting in front of her.

Diana crossed her arms on the toppings counter, far from the product of course, and looked at him. His own embarrassed blush had been chased away, and he'd turned his attention back to his yogurt. He'd doused the base, tart flavored yogurt with a helping of honey and chocolate chips with a couple cherries for color. Simple toppings for a simple sort of guy. She frowned though, when she caught sight of the back of his neck.

"Hey, your fuzzy thing is ripped," Diana said, walking around the counter. He looked over his shoulder as she fiddled with the edge of the neck piece. It was mostly covered by the fluff, but she could see where the leather strip that held it all together was torn. The fur around it had been ripped out, which is how she had noticed it in the first place. "How'd that happen?"

"It got caught on something," Harry said, shifting in place and staring hard at his yogurt cup. He seemed embarrassed for some reason. Diana wanted to hug him and make it all better, but instead she tuned in on his face turning red as Diana's fingers held onto the neck piece. She spun it a little, her finger catching the edge of his skin. Diana was tempted to tap it again, just for fun. Harry blurted, "It's not a big deal."

"Can you fix it?" Diana asked, letting go of the fur and moving her hand down to sit on his shoulder. She drew a circle there, happy to see his blush continue to grow. "Or will you need an entirely new one?"

"I can fix it," Harry blurted. He shoved a bite of yogurt into his mouth and leaned back into Diana's hand. She got the worst urge to lean over and kiss him. "It's not a big deal."

"I'm glad," Diana said. She poked his cheek and grinned, deciding friendly teasing was just what she needed to distract herself from tasting the yogurt on his tongue. "Though I won't lie, I bet you're pretty cute all scruffy, too."

Harry opened his mouth to reply, when their bubble was popped by an interruption.

"You two are adorable," Jolie said, leaning on her register. She had her chin in her hand, and a sparkle in her eyes. Diana jumped back from Harry, crossing her arms to avoid looking at either Harry or Jolie. How could she forget she was still at work? Jolie continued to grin, reveling in their embarrassment. "If I didn't know you two had at least gotten to first base, I would have given up on you two reaching home in this century."

"If you don't shut up, I'm going to break your legs and make sure you never get to a real first base again," Diana threatened, working her way back behind the counter. She turned on the sink and washed her hands, scrubbing harder than necessary until her hands were as pink as her face. "Ever. I'll make sure to hit the kneecap."

"No you won't."

No, she wouldn't. But that wasn't the point! "Just please, stop teasing."

"Okay, okay," Jolie said, holding up her hands. She turned to the still red Harry, the color clashing with his black and yellow ensemble. Jolie pressed her hands on the counter and pushed up straightening her arms so she could get a better view. Her smile was a tad more sincere, and far less teasing, when she continued. "You really should invite her over to your lace again, though. If only just to see that garden of yours."

"Yeah," Harry's voice cracked. He coughed and shoved down another bite of melted yogurt. The honey dripped off the spoon, spilling over the edge of the cup. Harry wiped it up with a napkin and swallowed heavily. "That'd be good. Really good. When, when are you free?"

"Most evenings," Diana answered. She pulled on a fresh pair of gloves and pretended her cheeks weren't flushed. "So whenever you are?"

"How about tonight?" Jolie grinned. "You two should go right after work."

"I'd need to clean up, so maybe tomorrow?" Harry offered quickly. "I just. I'd want to clean."

"Tomorrow's good," Diana said.

"Tomorrow then," Harry said, swallowing.

Another set of customers decided to walk through the door at that moment, and Diana and Harry's conversation was cut short. He waved as he left, and his cheeks still held a hint of blush as he walked past the window. Jolie continued grinning, her eyes sparkling in victory.

Diana ignored both her and the way butterflies started dancing in her stomach.

# CHAPTER 8

THE FIGURINES FIT into Harry's fairy garden better than Diana had anticipated.

She almost wished she'd gotten him a few more when she saw how much extra space there still was. Harry had set the few he'd gotten throughout the village though, so it wasn't as noticeable there were houses still missing residents. He'd placed most of them outside the doorways of houses, save for one. He had the daffodil fairy visiting the rose petal fairy, just to add a bit more character to the place.

Even if it was still sparse, they gave the little town a bit of life. *Though,* Diana thought to herself, stealing a glance at Harry's soft smile as he looked down at his garden. *It might be good there was still room for more residents at a later date.* Harry had mentioned this was the sort of project you worked on a little bit at a time.

Finishing it all at once would take the fun out of it.

Speaking of new additions, Diana was proud she noticed (and pointed out), the new house that had appeared on one of the fake hills since the last time she saw it.

"Princess helped me pick that one out," Harry said, reaching over and pointing to a spot on the side. A small bird had been painted into the wood, adding an extra bit of character. Harry swelled with pride. "She's gotten into painting lately."

"Good for her," Diana said. She crossed her arms on the edge of the flower box and exhaled. "I'm glad she's finding new things to do."

Their conversation lulled into silence after that, and as expected, they both ended up staring at the fairy garden for an extended period of time, neither willing to broach the subject of heading up the stairs and into

Harry's attic apartment.

Fairy gardens weren't the only things that were meant to be worked on a little bit at a time, were they?

But despite all of Diana's hopes to move their relationship to the next step, now that they had the opportunity, she found herself nervous. It was like she'd been transformed back into a terrified teen, scared that the second they went upstairs everything would change and this whole wonderful thing might end tomorrow if either of them made the wrong move. Diana didn't want to hurry to the end of this relationship any faster than Harry wanted to actually complete his garden.

Next to her, Harry tugged on his antennae, and she could see his chest moving up and down harder than usual with his nervous breathing. The breeze gently tugged on his wings and hair and Diana wondered if Harry was feeling the same way.

They were both way too old to be this nervous.

It was just his house. *Nothing has to happen today*, Diana reminded herself. *One step at a time.*

She was only going to see where Harry lived, and then maybe next time he could come into her house instead of just standing on her front porch when he picked her up or dropped her off. Even friends visited each other past the front door! But, she also didn't want to push. Just in case.

"You know, we don't have to go upstairs if you don't want to," Diana said, pressing her lips together. She kept her eyes glued to the tiny water wheel that spun lightly in the wind. She tapped his side with her elbow. "Jolie was mostly teasing."

"It's okay," Harry said, fiddling with his fingers. He looked at Diana for a few seconds before turning his gaze back on the fairy garden. "I mean, it's not really that big of a deal. It's just. I've only got the one room, so it's like I'm inviting you straight into my bedroom instead of my house and that makes me nervous even when it shouldn't. You know?"

"Like I said, I don't mind waiting," Diana said. She tucked her hair behind her ear and leaned on the fairy garden's siding. She reached over and flicked one of the fairies in the wing. "Maybe we could visit my house instead, first? I've got a living room and everything we could hang out in. I could make lemonade or something and we could watch a movie."

Harry laughed, rubbing the back of his hair. His hand lingered on the back of his neck, half of it lost in the fluff around his neck. His smile was crooked and cute; Diana's heart skipped a beat when he turned it toward her. "After we've already been here for an hour?"

"Yeah." Diana poked his arm. "Perfectly okay."

Harry took in a long breath and turned to Diana with a steady smile. The calm from him washed over her, and Diana took his hand when he offered it. He squeezed her fingers. "Want to see my room?"

"Sure," Diana said, lacing their fingers together.

The trip up the stairs took forever, and Diana just knew Harry had an awesome pair of legs under his jeans if he had to walk up and down four flights of stairs twice a day or more. She was nearly out of breath by the time they reached the top, and grateful he'd kept hold of her hand the entire time. Otherwise she probably would have given up and abandoned the journey around flight three. He pushed a key into the lock, biting his lip to stop from laughing at her lack of stamina. Diana smiled at the small metal honey bee that hung off the end of the keyring, momentarily forgetting her exhaustion. He pushed open the door at the same time he turned the key.

He flipped on a light, and Diana took one step past the threshold and into the attic apartment.

The room was smaller than she had expected. Drywall walls had been setup, creating a small finished room in the attic space that was a little larger than Diana's bedroom. She saw a small door to the back that she guessed was a restroom situated next to a kitchenette that took up a quarter of the far wall. His bed was in the opposite far corner, taking up a third of the space. The black comforter was folded neatly at the end, and the yellow sheets were tucked in under the mattress. Harry had a chest of drawers, a small standing wardrobe and a few bookshelves covered in various bee related knick-knacks spread out on the other two walls. A single light hung from the ceiling, and the pull chain for the fan was shaped like a piece of honeycomb.

"You weren't kidding when you said it was cozy," Diana said, strolling into the center to look around. She spotted the honeycomb barrette he wore on their first real date in a bowl on his chest of drawers and smiled. "I feel like it should be bigger considering how large this house is."

"I said it was a single room and small," Harry corrected. He closed his door and put his keys in a bowl next to the door that sat on top of a waist-high bookshelf. "The rest of the attic is storage and unfinished."

"Can you get to it from here?" Diana asked, glancing at the other door again. "I assumed that was a restroom, but is it a door to the rest of the attic?"

"No, it's a restroom," Harry laughed and took a seat on the edge of his bed. "It'd be kinda lousy if the attic apartment didn't have an en-suite, wouldn't it?"

"Tell me about it," Diana said, giggling back.

Harry shrugged and folded his hands in his lap. "There's a pull down stairwell on the third floor to get up to the rest of it. I sometimes help Princess and her mom bring down their Christmas decorations, which is mostly what's up there at this point. Everything else is just old storage no one looks at."

"Fun for you," Diana said. She pressed her fingers together, counted to ten in her head, and gave up. She took a seat next to Harry on his bed and leaned their shoulders together. "It's not so scary up here."

"I cleaned last night," Harry said, pushing his wing back so it didn't get crumbled on the bed as they sat. "Should have seen it before. You would have run screaming."

"It couldn't have been that bad," Diana said. She spread her legs out and crossed her legs at the ankles. Her jeans pulled up as she did so, and she caught Harry glance at it. Diana felt like one of those old Victorian ladies seducing men with the flash of their ankles and tried not to giggle. "Like I said, I've spent the night at Jolie's place."

Harry snorted. "I guess I'll take your word for it, then."

Diana tapped her fingers on the top of the bed sheet, and glanced around. She was a little surprised by the lack of monitors, television or computer. "No TV?"

"I've got a key to the main house," Harry said with a tiny shrug, flicking the wings on his back. "My boss has a theatre room, so if I really wanted to watch something, I'm free to use it. And if that's in use, she's got a recreation room with a couple televisions."

"Must be fun living above someone that loaded," Diana said, trying not to laugh. "Though somehow I can't see you abusing the privilege all that often."

"I try not to," Harry said. "She's a good woman."

*You're a good man,* Diana thought, but kept it in. She leaned on his arm and tugged on the metallic black fabric of his sleeves. "So, we made it upstairs. What now?"

"I'm not sure," Harry said, voice soft and unsure. He tilted his head toward her, and the tip of his antennae knocked against her hair. "What do you want to do?"

"Go in a circle of asking each other what we want to do while never actually admitting what we want to?" Diana asked, dropping her head on his shoulder. Harry stiffened for two seconds, before she heard the chuckles. He was laughing a full second later, and she shoved him over onto his side. "It wasn't that funny!"

"But it was," Harry said, rubbing the side of his eye and wiping away a small stream of tears. "It really was."

"Forgive me for saving us the time," Diana said, crossing her arms.

"You're forgiven," Harry said with a straight face, patting Diana on the thigh.

Kissing him seemed like the most appropriate response.

# CHAPTER 9

"YOU TWO ARE saints," Jolie said, popping another piece of gum in her mouth. She tapped her bat against her leg as she leaned on the chainlink fence. Her baseball uniform was still covered in red dirt from a slide earlier, and she made Diana want a shower just from looking at her. Jolie ignored the grit and game sweat like a champ, and continued to wait on her turn to bat. "I can't believe you spent two hours in his room and didn't get past first base."

"You act like it's a race," Diana huffed, watching the field. Jolie's teammates were in the lead, but only by two runs. Diana couldn't tell if she was grateful or not that the game wasn't a close one. The bright side? Their team was winning. The opposite? Jolie didn't need to pay one hundred percent attention to the game, and could instead spend her free time commenting on Diana's love life. "I've been out of the game for years, and I think relationships are new to him in general. Nothing wrong with us taking our time."

"It's been over two months since you started dating," Jolie huffed. She pushed off the fence and swung her bat back. She swung it forward in the air, hard enough that the air practically snapped around it. She kept up the practice batting, aiming hard at a ball only she could see. "And kissing is as far as you've gotten, and from what I can tell, you only use tongue once in a while. Like when you're on his bed. Poor guy is either a saint or scared to death of you."

"Or he could be shy, or self conscious, or he wants to wait, or a whole bunch of other things," Diana said, crossing her arms. It didn't help she was having a hard time reading how far he wanted to go herself. Sure he asked for the first kiss, but he didn't ask for more than that. Did that mean he wasn't interested in more, or that he couldn't tell if Diana wanted more? "And it's not like I've been asking or we've ever really sat down to discuss it, so he's probably just being considerate."

Diana paused, thinking that over. She pointed through the fence, straight at her pushy friend. "Which is pretty nice, if you ask me. It's hard to find a guy like that!"

"Do you want him to do more?" Jolie asked, popping a bubble. She swung the bat again, over and over in a steady rhythm. The next person in line stepped up to bat, and Jolie paused only to make sure she didn't need to head to the waiting circle. "Because if you do, you should probably tell him."

"I guess," Diana said. She watched the next batter strike out and huffed. "Looks like you're on the field."

"Defense it is," Jolie said. She smiled over her shoulder as she dropped her bat into the basket in the dugout. She grabbed her glove and ran away from the fence, ready to head to her post on the pitcher's mound.

Diana took a few steps back and sat on the bleacher. She tugged her baseball cap down, shielding her eyes from the sun and settled in to watch the game more comfortably. Diana always preferred these casual community games over going to the stadium to see the pro leagues with Jolie. She didn't hate the sport, but Diana just couldn't get into it the way her friend did. The only real point of watching the game was to see Jolie play, and she could only do that here. It was only a matter of time though before Jolie got noticed, and then Diana really would be going to the pros to see her best friend dominate the field.

That girl could play.

Twelve pitches later, and Jolie was back by the fence with a wink to grab her bat. The opposing team was scowling, but their irritation only fueled Jolie's ego. Diana laughed as Jolie skipped over to wait for her next at bat near the current batter. She looked ready to go; like she knew exactly what she wanted.

Diana envied her when it came down to it.

She did want to go further with Harry. Maybe not quite to the point of getting out of her pants, but a little further. Diana shifted in her seat. Far enough to feel his fingertips on her stomach, or on her back. Maybe his mouth on her collarbone, and her own hands on his waist. Feel his weight press her into the couch cushion as he crawled on top of her. His wings hanging off his back and near her shoulders when she—

A loud crack filled the air, yanking Diana out of her daydream. She watched the ball fly toward the outfield and reminded herself she was there to pay attention to her friend and the game, no matter how much Jolie wanted to talk about it. She breathed out and watched the players. The batter made it to base, and now it was Jolie's turn. Diana watched her step up and crossed her fingers. Jolie had her life together, or at least as together as it was ever going to get. Maybe it was time Diana did, too.

But she could leave it a little up to fate.

"Whatever base Jolie makes it to," Diana whispered to herself, "is how far I'll ask to go with Harry when I see him tonight."

Jolie gave herself a last few practice swings before she settled at the plate. The first pitch flew, and Jolie didn't swing. Diana straightened in her seat as the umpire called "Strike!" She bit her lip at the second pitch. Jolie swung; a miss. Strike two. Diana held her breath as Jolie readjusted her stance, leaning forward until Diana was on the edge of the seat and her hand grabbed the fence. She breathed in, and got ready for the third.

The pitch.

The swing.

Jolie knocked it straight under the left outfielder's feet. He stumbled over himself tripping to turn and grab the ball as Jolie shot away from the plate like fire was at her heels. Diana jumped out of her seat, cheering loudly with the ten or twenty other spectators and yelled as Jolie slid into second before the ball could make it to the base.

Diana fell back into her seat, breathing hard and heart pounding from more than Jolie's impressive move. Her face split into a grin and she gave a little fist pump to her side, thanking fate and her talented friend.

Second base it was!

There were too many stairs at Harry's place.

Diana wheezed as she fell back on his bed, hand on her stomach. No matter how many times she climbed that blasted set of wooden steps, she was always winded by the time they reached the top. It was only three and a half floors worth of stairs. It shouldn't be this bad. Diana groaned and rubbed her eyes. It was time to face facts: She was out of shape. Maybe Diana would take Jolie up on those invites to go exercising with her every morning. Harry laughed at her misery as he dropped his keys in the bowl, and Diana threw a pillow at him.

"Do you want something to drink?" Harry asked, leaning over her, his head tilted and antennae bouncing. He held a finger up in a lecture-like pose. "After a work out, it's important to stay hydrated."

"You keep that up and we're not making out," Diana lied. They both knew that the only reason they bothered to come upstairs was to kiss and cuddle. All the interesting things to do otherwise were out in the yard, or downstairs in the theatre room. Harry pressed his lips together with a smirk and rolled his eyes, openly calling her bluff. And then she got an idea. A brilliant idea that might put her real plan into action. Diana rolled on her side, pressing her lips together. "I mean it. I won't kiss you."

"Oh?" Harry said, asking politely and playing along better than she was expecting. "Was that a threat, Ms. Winded?"

"That's it!" Diana said, kicking her shoes off. She pulled her legs up on the bed, and rolled onto her back. She pulled her knees up, dragging her foot back on the blanket. "No kisses from me to you."

Harry took the bait and came closer until his knees were pressed against the side of the mattress. He crossed his arms over his chest, and hummed. Diana spread her legs apart, just enough to catch his eye and grinned. Harry moved his arm up to tug on the furry fluff around his neck, wrapping a few strands around his finger. "That sounded like an awfully specific threat."

"It might have been worded that way for a reason, yes," Diana said, patting the side of the bed. He sat on the side, and that wouldn't do for Diana's beating heart. She tugged his arm across her body until his hand hit the mattress on the other side of her, and pulled until he took the hint and settled between her knees. His shoes were still on, and Diana didn't feel like giving him a chance to take them off. Instead, she put her hands on his thighs. Confusion and red showed on his face at the same time as his situation began to process. "I had something in mind."

"Oh?" Harry asked. Diana stared hard at the rise and fall of his chest under the yellow and black stripes, the nervous breathing she'd grown so fond of. They'd been close before, but never been like this. Never with their hips flush, and one of them on their back. Diana grinned when he asked, "Like what?"

"I was thinking you could kiss me," Diana said, keeping her own heart beat under control. Her hips begged to move but she kept them still. One step at a time, and she wanted second, not home. She tapped her lips and said, "But not here."

"Oh," Harry said, swallowing. The gravel in his voice increased with his needy breaths, and Diana nearly broke her word and kissed him first. Harry dared to touch her hip and asked, "Where?"

"Here." Diana pointed to her collarbone, under the fabric of her t-shirt. Harry watched her finger as she moved it down an inch. "Though you might need to take my shirt off to get there."

"Is that okay?" Harry whispered, his fingers tightening on her hip. Even with the contacts blocking his eyes, Diana could tell he was searching her face for permissions Diana had yet to give out right.

Diana picked up his hands and put them higher on her waist, before putting her arms above her head. She could feel her heart threatening to jump out of her ribs as his fingers dug into the fabric and pushed it up. He exposed her belly button and he stopped, his hands trembling. Diana gave him the final push, her own voice feeling as gritty as his as she said, "I'd really like it if you took off my shirt, Harry."

She had expected him to do it quick in his nervousness, like ripping off a band-aid. But instead, he surprised her in the best way. Harry kissed her belly, before pushing her shirt up another few inches. Diana sucked in a breath, and twisted her hip on the bed as he kept revealing skin inch by inch. A new trail of kisses followed until he found the center of her breasts. She could barely see his face with the bunch of t-shirt in her vision, and she groaned when he licked the side of her breast.

"Don't remember asking for that," Diana gasped, pulling her own shirt off the rest of the way and tossing it on the floor.

"Read in between the lines," Harry said, a tiny smile tugging on his mouth. He pressed his face into her neck; his hand trailed up her ribs. "Is that okay?"

"You keep that sort of improv up," Diana said, tugging on the back of his hair when he licked her throat and her hip jerked. "And you'll get my bra off today, too."

Harry laughed into the top of her chest, falling on Diana and knocking the breath out of her lungs. He was heavy and wonderful and she found herself laughing with him. He kissed the first place Diana pointed to, and she rolled her eyes and grabbed his head tugging him up.

"I lied earlier," Diana said. She tugged him down and kissed him hard. He welcomed it, and their teeth knocked as they struggled with this new, horizontal pose. "It's hard not to kiss you."

"And I was just getting to like kissing new places," Harry said, bumping their noses together.

"You'll just have to map them out for later," Diana said, tugging his hand up onto her breast. Only his thumb touched skin with the rest of his fingers deep into the fabric of her bra, but that was okay when their hips were together and she had all of him to herself. "Think you can handle that?"

"Yeah," Harry said, dropping into another kiss and bucking his hips up.

Diana wrapped her arms around his shoulders, grabbing at the fluff around his neck and clinging to his shirt. She squeezed her thighs together around him, happy with the warmth and the wet of his mouth locked with hers. His hands wandered to her back, fingers under her bra strap and Diana moaned into his mouth.

The door slammed open a second later, jerking them both apart.

"Harry!" Princess shouted, helping herself into the room. "I know you're home, so stop ignoring my—"

She shrieked when she spotted the two on the bed.

"Princess?" Harry asked, sitting up. Diana covered her face and groaned, willing herself not to throw something at the intruder. *Of all the times for her to show up.* Harry, tugged up the side of his bed sheet to cover Diana's top, but she sat up with a huff and ignored it. It wasn't anything Princess hadn't seen before, and Diana was still wearing her bra. Harry winced as he looked away and focused on Princess. "Did you need something?"

"You," Princess said, pointing. She stopped and her entire face flushed like a strawberry. Princess' hand shook on the door knob, still gripping it tightly. "Where's her shirt?"

"On the floor," Diana said, covering her eyes. Princess was what? Eighteen? Nineteen? She had to know what was going on. The fact she hadn't left yet was the most annoying bit about all of this. Most people would have left the second they walked in with a quick "Excuse me!" Though Diana couldn't really blame her for not wanting to trudge down those stairs again so soon after all the work to get up here. "What do you want?"

Princess stomped her foot, or at least that's what it sounded like, and growled. "None of your business."

Diana pulled her hand down and glared at the intruder. She and

Harry had been dating for months. This jealousy, or sibling overprotectiveness, or whatever the hell that girl's hang up was had gotten old weeks ago.

She almost said something, but Harry beat her to it: "Princess, we're still in the middle of a date, if you don't mind. Is what you needed important, or can it wait until tomorrow?"

Princess sucked in a heavy breath and pressed her lips together. She looked at the floor with watery eyes, and for a few seconds Diana almost felt bad for her. Almost. Eventually, Princess shuffled one of her feet back and forth, and her grip on the doorknob loosened. "It can wait. Sorry for intruding."

She dashed out of the room, slamming the door loudly behind her.

"That could have gone better," Harry mumbled, collapsing on the bed next to Diana. He wrapped his arm around her waist and rested his head on her shoulder. Harry buried his nose into her neck and squeezed. "Probably should have remembered to lock the door."

"Not your fault she's rude," Diana said, patting his back.

"Still should have locked it," Harry muttered. "I have every other time we've been up here. Figures this would be the one time I forgot."

"Again," Diana said, petting his hair. "She's old enough to know better, or should at least be old enough to know when it's time to leave instead of gawk."

"She's used to coming up whenever she wants," Harry said, rubbing a small circle on her stomach. Diana concentrated on the warm breathes against her neck and his weight that pressed her into the mattress. It wasn't quite what she had been hoping for earlier, but the intimacy of it was still so warm. Harry pressed his thumb into her side, tracing her hip bone. "I told her she was always welcome if I was home, so she's probably still not used to having someone else around. Gets lonely downstairs with her mom working all the time."

"Then maybe she should find more friends," Diana said. "Or learn how to share."

Harry chuckled and squeezed Diana tighter, kissing the side of her neck in a light brush. "She's already taking this whole thing way better than I could have ever expected. So consider yourself lucky."

"I'd hate to see her taking this badly," Diana said.

"Same," Harry said. He snickered into her side, and dropped his hand. "You should have seen her when her mom was dating."

"I'll take a raincheck on that."

Harry snorted, and buried his face into her neck. She felt him breathe in, and she shifted her leg up, resting her thigh against Harry's waist. He didn't move, not even to get more comfortable. The man felt heavier than he had before, but in that drained and tired way that Diana recognized from a too long day at work or getting off the phone after a fight with her parents. Princess had killed the mood hard enough that it was going to stay dead, hadn't she? But then again, she wouldn't want to make out after a family member caught her in the act, either.

Diana huffed and rolled over, shifting until she hugged his face into her chest instead of her neck. That was fine. No point in bringing back the mood if he wasn't feeling it. That playfulness from earlier had to have come from somewhere, so it had to come back. Diana grinned into his hair, squeezing his side. There'd be a next time. For sure.

She yawned into his hair. If they weren't going to make out, an afternoon nap might be just what the doctor ordered. "I feel sorry for you after I leave."

Harry nuzzled into her chest, and Diana smiled.

Things would be okay.

# CHAPTER 10

JOLIE WAS STILL laughing.

Diana refilled the chocolate chip dish and rolled her eyes. One day she would learn not to tell Jolie things about her love life. And another day she'd learn to stop telling herself blatant lies. But neither of those days were today. "It really isn't as funny as you keep making it out to be."

"No, it is," Jolie said in-between the gasps of breath. Her ribs must hurt from all the laughing. Jolie had already doubled over onto the counter and had her forehead dropped onto the top of their register. "It's going to kill me. I'm going to die of laughter and it's your fault."

"It could have happened to anyone," Diana said. She dropped the giant tub of chocolate chips back onto the push cart. Reaching for the sprinkles next, she hauled it up onto the counter. "I mean, who hasn't had their younger sibling walk in on them once or twice?"

"You don't even have a younger sibling," Jolie said, raising her eyebrows. "So how would you know?"

"Television?"

"Probably good enough," Jolie said, still snickering. Diana longed for a customer, if just to break up being the center of Jolie's attention for a few minutes. "But still, it is kinda funny. You finally get in there ready to slide home, and you're called out by the ump."

"We talked about baseball puns," Diana said, pulling the scoop out of the tub with a generous portion of the multicolored topping. She dumped it into its tub with more force than necessary. "And I was going for second, thank you."

"Sure you were," Jolie said, popping a piece of gum into her mouth. She tapped her hands on the counter in a tiny percussion beat, ever bursting with energy. "The way things were sounding, you two were going to get farther than that. Maybe it's a good thing Princess crashed your party."

"Very funny," Diana said. She finished up the last of the topping restocking and shoved the cart back into the store room.

She would have felt better though, if Jolie didn't have a point.

Things had gotten a little more heated than Diana was expecting, not that she'd been complaining at the time. But that next step was a bit of a big one, and as much as she liked Harry, she still didn't know too much about him. She didn't know anything about his family, or if he had any other friends, or if he had hobbies outside of the fairy garden or the bee thing.

Heck, Diana had been dating him for all this time now and she still had no clue why he dressed like a bee even if she had gotten used to it.

"I wonder if those contacts hurt," Diana said under her breath, forgetting where she was for the moment. She leaned on the counter, tempted to steal a tiny cup of yogurt while the shop was empty. Anything to keep her occupied.

"If what hurts?" Jolie asked, nudging her side with her elbow. "Got to speak up if you want a conversation."

"Harry's contacts," Diana said, waving her hand up toward her eyes. "He's got those sclera ones, and I wonder if they hurt. I mean, I heard you're not supposed to wear those things very long and I've never seen him take them off."

Even when they'd taken that nap, he'd kept them in. Diana was pretty sure sleeping in regular contacts was near agony, let alone those big ones.

"Maybe he takes them off when no one's around?" Jolie asked, scrunching her nose. "I mean, it's not bad for his eyes or anything is it?"

"I don't know," Diana said, holding her cheek in her hand.

"You could always ask him," Jolie said. She shrugged and popped a bubble. "If you're worried about him, it can't be too bad."

"Maybe."

"Just ask him," Jolie said. "And hey, you might get a peek at what color eyes Mr. Tall and Blond really has under there."

Diana nodded and crossed her arms on the counter. She stared at the container of chocolate chips and wondered if his eyes were brown. Diana rubbed her cheek and tried to get her thoughts back to work. "That would be something."

It wasn't until three or four customers later that Diana remembered questioning Harry about his costume usually got the man to freeze up. He never outright avoided the questions, but they did make him uncomfortable.

Like the time Diana had asked how he got his shirt on over his wings, and how he was wearing them in the first place. As it turned out, the answer was a rather impressive harness made of soft leather straps under his shirt that had a zipper down the back. He'd modified all his shirts so they fit neatly around the wings, and that was true dedication to his daily costume (and a hint that Harry had some sewing skills under his belt).

However, the whole time he'd explained, and the quick glance Diana had gotten of his harness, were spoken to the floor as Harry fidgeted. He avoided eye contact, and despite the fact that Diana was impressed with how he got the whole system to work and look so flawless, he still seemed embarrassed.

She'd made a personal note not to ask any more.

Which made asking about the contacts a bit of a dilemma.

Diana didn't like making Harry feel embarrassed or self conscious. Frankly, it was the last thing she ever wanted to do, and now that she'd gotten so used to the costume, she barely noticed it.

She bit the edge of her finger, and hummed. But what if the contacts were hurting him? There had to be some reason he wore that costume all the time, something dedicated, and did that mean he ignored other things about himself? What if those stupid contacts were hurting him?

Diana ruffled her own hair and groaned. There had to be someone else she could ask. Someone who knew Harry pretty well. Or at least well enough to know if he ever took the contacts out to give his eyes a rest.

But who?

She stopped, hating herself even as the name popped into her head.

Diana knew who she could ask.

"I'm not apologizing," Princess hissed, slamming a jar of honey on the shelf. She put the next one up from the basket in her hand and refused to turn around. "Just so you know."

"Not going to ask you to," Diana said. She rubbed the back of her neck and wandered closer to the shelf. Harry had left early for a doctor's appointment, which made this the perfect opportunity to corner Princess without distraction. "I just had a question, and I knew you'd have the answer."

Hopefully, anyway.

"What do you want, then?" Princess asked, huffing and continuing to stack the shelf. Her hair was pulled back today, and her shoulders were dropped. She looked defeated. Despite wishing that she could, Diana felt no joy in her victory. Making teenagers sad just wasn't in her, no matter how much of a brat they could be. Princess kept stacking, her shoulders stiff and eyes hurt. "Because frankly, I don't like talking to you."

"I had a question about Harry," Diana said. "And since I didn't want to hurt his feelings, I figured I'd ask you."

"If you think it'll hurt his feelings, then why do you want to know in the first place?" Princess asked.

"I'm worried about something, and if it's not actually an issue, I don't want to bring it up and upset him on accident," Diana said. She leaned on the counter, rubbing the arm of her sleeve. She only had about ten more minutes before they'd miss her at the shop, so hopefully Princess cooperated sooner than later. "That's all."

Princess put down her box of honey on the counter and spun around on the back of her foot. She crossed her arms and held her chin up. "What is it?"

"Do you know if he takes out his contacts once in a while?" Diana asked, tapping against the side of her cheek. "I heard keeping those sclera contacts in for long hours is painful and bad for your eyes."

"Oh," Princess said, her grip on her own arms loosening. She sighed and shrugged. "Yeah, I asked him about that before. He says it varies from person to person, and he's okay with them. No vision problems or pain, so I think he's good."

"So he only takes them out at night?" Diana asked, rubbing the back of her neck. "Huh."

"Didn't say that," Princess huffed. She glanced to the side and shrugged. "He takes them off when he gets home and knows he's not going anywhere. Sometimes I'll catch him without them if I surprise him with a visit, but he doesn't like it."

"Alright then," Diana said, clapping her hands together. "That answer that."

She paused for a moment, unsure of how to continue, and settled for a reserved. "Thank you for answering. That helped me out a lot."

Princess shuffled, and touched the shelf with her hands. She watched Diana from the corner of her eye, wary and tired. "Do you really like him?"

If this had been a few months ago, back when they were first dating, Diana might have had a hard time answering that. But now, now the words came all too easily:

"Yeah, I do."

"Okay then," Princess said.

She went back to stacking the shelves with a determined look on her face, and Diana considered herself dismissed.

Well, up until Princess turned around and pointed at her, "But you had better remember that Harry is basically my big brother. So if you hurt him, I'll make your life hell."

"Duly noted, Ms. Cliché Threat." Diana laughed, helping herself out the door.

She was about a block away when Princess slammed the door open and shouted down the street, "Just because it's cliché doesn't mean it's not true! You watch it! This is not over!"

Diana giggled the entire way back to the shop.

# CHAPTER 11

DIANA HAD SETTLED into her love seat with a cup of tea and the remote, ready for a late night of binge watching the last few episodes of that baseball drama Jolie had leant her last week. One of these days Diana would have to admit that Jolie was breaking her down into becoming a baseball fan, but that day would not be today nor tomorrow. Or ever. Even if Diana did admit she was growing fond of the sport, she would never tell Jolie. She just didn't have it in her to give her friend that kind of satisfaction.

But, at least the show was good. There was plenty to watch and pick apart when it came to the characters and plot even without the baseball portions, which was probably its biggest saving grace. Otherwise, Diana would have preferred to watch old recordings of baseball games. Better to watch the real thing than fiction if there was nothing else but the game right? Plus, she knew Jolie had a rather extensive collection of recorded baseball games ranging from historical archives to last year's Major League games if she wanted to watch them. However, Diana was no where near enough of a closet fan to want to watch them. Diana would stick to the live community games, thank you very much.

And only if Jolie was in them.

Diana frowned, sipping tea from her cup; she wasn't a baseball fan.

The doorbell rang, saving Diana from her miniature existential crisis that she was becoming a genuine sports fan. She put her tea on the coffee table, and grabbed her robe to wrap it around her nightgown before approaching the door. She looked through the peep hole, and saw a familiar face standing on her stoop.

She opened the door and hummed, "You know, I didn't give stock to the whole think of the devil and he'll appear thing, but I was honestly just thinking about you, Jolie."

"Aw, I'm flattered," Jolie said, tapping her bat up and down on her shoulder. She looked like she'd just come from practice, her uniform still stained with dirt and grass. Jolie frowned heavily for a second before turning her head to the side. She dropped her bat and said, "Oh, no you don't."

Before Diana could respond, she yanked Harry into view, and said, "This belongs to you."

"Harry?" Diana asked, and gaped. He clutched a ripped section of his wing to his chest with his antennae headband, and his gaze was locked on the ground. There was a large purple bruise forming across the side of his face, and a black eye on the opposite side. His shirt was ripped at the top of the sleeve, exposing the harness he wore underneath for his wings. The tall man hunched his shoulders in, and he looked positively miserable. "What happened? Are you okay?"

"Found him getting his ass handed to him by some losers on my way home from practice," Jolie said, popping a gum bubble. She had a death grip on Harry's arm and shrugged. "I scared them off with my bat and they ran like chickens. He's not bad enough to go to the hospital, but like, I couldn't let him go home like this right?"

Harry remained silent, his shoulders trembling.

"So, here you go!" Jolie said, shoving Harry though the doorway. "Might want to clean him up a bit. I'll see you at work, tomorrow!"

And with that, Jolie saluted and tapped down the sidewalk to her car, throwing the bat into the back seat onto her equipment bag. She waved, leaving Harry alone in Diana's living room. The poor man looked mortified from head to toe, and Diana wasn't sure if she shouldn't just drive him home. Jolie had good intentions, but this might have been too far.

"Hey," Diana said, tugging on the edge of his sleeve. Harry grunted, but looked in her direction. She smiled and rubbed his arm. She reached over and gently took his broken wing piece and snapped headband from his arms and put them on the kitchen table behind her. Harry's shoulders slumped, but he still didn't say anything. Diana tried not to worry too much, and decided to go ahead and just take the lead. "Let's get you cleaned up, okay? You've got dirt shoved into your cheek."

"Alright," Harry said. His gravely voice was hoarse, like he'd been crying a few moments earlier.

Her heart ached, hearing such a defeated thing from him and Diana couldn't help herself. She leaned up and kissed him on the cheek. "You know where the bathroom is. I'll find some extra towels, so help yourself to a shower. But don't be mad if the hot water goes out in the middle, because I took a rather long one before you got here."

A small smile graced his face as he snorted, and Diana felt some of the tension leave her shoulders.

Harry had a towel draped over his head and had sunken into Diana's love seat where she had been earlier. His foreleg rested against the table next to her forgotten cup of tea. She replaced it with a fresh cup of Earl Gray with a generous portion of honey and milk stirred into the cup. He took it gratefully and sipped. Diana tried to ignore the way the bruise moved against his skin as he took a drink.

"Do you want to talk about what happened?" Diana asked, helping herself to a seat next to him. She pulled a leg under her as she sat sideways on the couch, leaning on the back. He flinched for a second, but didn't drop his cup. Diana back tracked. "But we don't have to if you're upset."

"No, it's okay." Harry sunk further into the couch, his remaining wing crinkled under him. He had redressed after his shower before Diana had the chance to offer him a robe or to find him some other sort of clothes. It almost hurt her to see him wearing his ripped clothes again after taking the time to get the rest of him clean.

It absolutely hurt Diana to see his wings folded and ripped after all the care he usually put into moving it aside when he sat down. Harry cradled his tea cup and shrugged. "I was out for a walk and they wanted someone to pick on. I'm an easy target so they went for it. Not much more to it than that."

"You must have been pretty far away from home," Diana said, dropping her head on the back of the couch. She wanted to put it on his shoulder, but didn't want to crowd him. "I mean, the nearest house to you is like half a mile away."

Harry snorted, and slumped further down in the couch, knocking his knees into the table. He tilted his head back and to the side. The contacts were in the way, but Diana knew their eyes were locked. "There's a path behind my house a bit in the woods. Community project. The walk goes all the way down to the park and athletic fields Jolie uses. It's a nice walking trail if you've got time for it."

"Huh, never knew that was back there," Diana said, poking his arm. "Didn't want to make the walking trail a date?"

"Usually when we get to my place, you either want to see the garden or my room, so I tend to be distracted," Harry said. He pressed his lips together and a smile threatened to escape, though his bad night kept it at bay. "Not that I have any complaints about that."

"Good," Diana said. She scooted over and dropped her head on his shoulder, and wrapped her hands around his arm. "I like distracting you."

She hummed and laughed. "Still, I had no idea that Jolie's field was so close to your house. I wonder why I never put that together? I go to both places enough that I probably should have picked up they were in the same area."

"They're in opposite directions and there are a lot of woods," Harry said. "It's easy to get turned around. Besides, it's a long path. It's a good hour jog to the field."

"Well, that makes me feel better," Diana said. "Little surprised you didn't tell Jolie where you lived though. Considering how close it was, she could have dropped you off at home instead."

"I did," Harry said, falling over sideways. Diana squeaked as they fell on the couch together. He hugged her to himself, and his face fell in her shoulder. He mumbled into her skin. "She said I couldn't go home alone with a black eye."

"She can be awfully smart when it comes to those sort of matters," Diana said, wiggling her arm around his back to dig into the back of his hair. She pet there, digging her fingers into his scalp. His body relaxed and she hummed. "How'd Jolie manage to scare them off anyway? I mean, you're a big guy, so I can't see a group willing to pick a fight with you being that cared of someone half your size."

"She left out the part in her story where she had the rest of her team behind her," Harry said, snorting. "They heard her yelling and showed up with their own bats. The jerks that jumped me made a run for it."

"So this must have happened right at the lot," Diana said. "Wow, bold guys to pick a fight there."

"Like I said," he sighed. "Easy target. I think I was too tempting to pass up."

"Does," Diana started. She pressed her lips together and turned to hug him tighter. "Does this sort of thing happen a lot?"

"Not as much as you're thinking," Harry said. He drummed his fingers on her waist and blew out a heavy breath. "But enough that you'll probably see it happen again. Truth be told, you've already seen it before."

"You mean the at the restaurant when they threw the napkin at you?" Diana asked, thinking hard for when she could have seen Harry in a state of disarray. Nothing came to mind that was even remotely close to him getting jumped in the woods. "Or something else?"

Harry scooted up on the couch and dropped his head on top of Diana's. He reached up and tugged his furry collar. "Remember when you noticed it was torn?"

"You said it was caught on something," Diana said. She snuggled into his side and winced. "Oh. Someone pulled it, didn't they?"

"Yeah. Not the worst they've ever done, but it still hurt," Harry said. He exhaled, nuzzling into Diana's hair as he leaned further on her. She was happy to take the extra weight. So close, she could almost hear the beat of his heart. Harry mumbled, "It's been going on since I was a kid, so I wouldn't expect it to stop now that I'm an adult."

Diana squeezed his arm. "Come on. You and I are going to get a bowl of ice cream and then go to bed. It's been a long day, right?"

Harry laughed, taking her hand and playing with the fingers. "You still have that honey topping?"

"Yup," Diana said. She sat up and kissed him on the head before going to the kitchen.

Diana thought she would be more nervous about the first time she and Harry shared the bed for the night, but with the evening he'd had and the exhaustion weighing them both down, the total lack of expectations made it less of an issue than if she'd invited him to stay the night a day ago.

Finding him something to sleep in was more of a hassle than sharing the bed, honestly.

Settling on one of Diana's over-sized sleep shirts (which funny enough was still almost too small for Harry) and his boxers, the pajama matter had been settled.

What was surprising, was just how naked Harry looked without his antennae, wings, and that furry collar he loved so much. It was almost like ten or twenty pounds of weight had been stripped from him; like he was an entirely different person. All that he had left of his costume were the slight bruises from his harness that she could see through the thin t-shirt and his contacts.

Concerned, for the later observation, Diana poked his cheek just under his eye. "You're not sleeping in your contacts, right?"

"Oh," Harry said. He reached up and ran his hand through his hair. The hand passed all the way from the front to the back, without obstruction from his headband and it was almost weird to see. He laughed and licked the side of his lip. "Forgot I was wearing them."

He scooted off the edge of her bed and dug into his pants pockets. Harry pulled out a contact lens case and opened it up. Diana watched his back as he tugged out the contacts, placing them into the little wells of liquid. He twisted the case lid back on quick a quick wrist flip, and didn't move, his back still toward her. Harry turned the case over, and Diana had a feeling she knew what caused that slight tremor in his fingers.

"I can turn off the lights now, if it bothers you," she said, trying to be diplomatic. "If you're not ready, I mean."

His shoulders fell, and Diana could almost map the tension as it drained out of his body. He pushed the contact case back into his pocket and rested his hands on the back of his head. Diana pulled her knees up on the bed and waited quietly, seeing no reason to rush him.

Harry laughed, a burst of relieved joy, and turned his head around. Diana met the most gorgeous pair of honey-brown eyes she'd ever seen, and if that color was one-hundred percent fitting she didn't know what was. He rubbed the back of his neck and shrugged, "Well, you're going to see them at some point. Might as well get it out of the way now."

"I hope you don't mind me saying," Diana started as Harry collapsed next to her on the bed. He rolled on his side, facing her and looked up. She bit her lip, and poked his cheek. "But with eyes that pretty, I'm a little surprised you hide them all the time."

"Costume doesn't seem complete without the contacts," Harry said, rubbing his palm back and forth on Diana's sheet. She stretched her legs out, and lay next to him. Harry reached up and tugged on a bit of her hair, wrapping it around her finger. "Doesn't quite feel right."

"It's weird seeing you without the costume," Diana muttered. She scooted closer and tucked herself neatly into his side. Head on his shoulder, she patted her hand on his ribs, noting the heat of his body. "You almost look like a totally different person."

"It's probably odd I'm glad to hear you say that, isn't it?" Harry said. He wrapped his arms around her and squeezed. "Because I feel like a different person when I'm not wearing it all. I don't. I don't feel like me."

Diana hugged him, not sure how to respond to that.

Harry turned and pressed his face into her hair. His next words were a whisper, "I'm sorry. I know that's weird."

"Not as much as you'd think," Diana admitted. She chuckled into his shoulder and nuzzled it. "As far as deep dark secrets go, you could have had much worse, I think."

"I'm really lucky," Harry admitted. He laughed and hugged her so tightly to his chest that Diana wasn't sure she could breathe. "So damn lucky."

"I could say the same," Diana said. She rubbed his side and reached down to pull the blankets up. "Come on, weirdo. Let's get some sleep or we'll both be late for work tomorrow."

A few minutes later, after the lights were off and Diana felt her breath slowing down in rhythm with his, he whispered into the top of her head. "Do you still want to know?"

"Know what?" Diana mumbled.

"Why I wear the costume?"

She kissed the front of his shirt and squeezed him back. "Would you still be willing to tell me in the morning?"

"Yeah, I think so," Harry said, and she could almost feel the smile in her hair. "Why?"

"Because I'm half asleep and you've already had an exhausting day," Diana said. "Save it for coffee."

Harry laughed into her hair and tugged the blankets tighter around them. She settled with him and breathed out, feeling the sleep take over every inch of her. Her sturdy pillow mumbled into her hair, "Coffee it is."

Waking up with Harry was something Diana could more than get used to.

He was warm, sturdy, and apparently an early riser. As Diana sat up, yawning deeply into her hands, she looked to the side to see Harry, contacts in and changed back into his clothes, just in time for him to hand her a cup of coffee. She took the mug and sipped it, glad that he remembered how she liked it.

Harry sat on the edge of the bed, his own cup twisting in his hand and he rested against Diana's raised knees. "So, coffee talk?"

"Coffee talk," Diana said. She nudged her knee against his back and grinned around the cup. "I know last night was sort of emotional, so just remember you don't have to say anything until you want to."

"I want to."

There was so much conviction and need in his voice that Diana found herself greedy for every inch of information Harry could give her. She put her coffee cup on the table, and wrapped her arms around her knees, closing the distance between the two of them. "So tell me."

"It started when I was one," Harry said, still twisting his cup of coffee in a small circle. Without the rest of his costume on, he still looked smaller than he was supposed to be. "My mom made me the best little bumblebee costume you've ever seen. It was for some children's Halloween, sorry 'Harvest Day', thing at church and my costume won. It was great."

"I bet you were cute," Diana grinned.

"I've got pictures somewhere," Harry said.

"You will have to share."

"Okay, but moving on. As it turned out, I liked that costume as much as anyone else did and my first word when I was two turned out to be 'honey bee.' So, mom decided to make me a honey bee costume that year."

"And let me guess, you got a new bee costume every year after?" Diana asked.

"Yup," Harry grinned. "Got pictures of those too and you saved me a bit of story. My sixth one was particularly cute, because I was a little blue carpenter bee."

"Okay," Diana said. She scooted around until she sat side by side with Harry and leaned on his arm. She rested her head on his shoulder, encouraging him to keep going. "And your Halloween theme graduated to full time when?"

"When I was fourteen, I wasn't doing so well at school," Harry said. He leaned on Diana and pressed his lips together. "Socially, I mean. And

I just couldn't figure it out. I wasn't bad looking, and I stayed out of people's way, so I didn't understand why this one group of kids wanted to pick on me all the time. They said I was weird and all sorts of names I don't really care to repeat.

"So when Halloween came around, I put on my costume like I always did, and I felt great. I always felt good in my costume, you know? It was just so *me*. And no one could really make fun of me, because even when they did, the words just washed off. I just felt that good in my honey bee outfit."

Harry paused, and took a sip from his coffee. His hands trembled a bit, and Diana wondered how much he was leaving out. She hugged his arm tighter. "So then what happened?"

"My mom reminded it me it was my last year to go trick or treating," Harry laughed. "Technically, our area capped it at thirteen, but I looked young enough that I could still pass. But I wouldn't get away with it at fifteen and the thought of never getting to wear my costume again scared me. I was terrified that I would never get to feel that good about myself again.

"As dumb as that sounds, as a fourteen year old kid who hated himself every day of the year but Halloween, it was unacceptable.

"So the day after, I wore my costume to school, minus the wings and the headband to meet dress code," Harry said. He dropped his head on Diana's and laughed. "My contacts freaked everyone out, and I got teased like hell for the fuzzy collar, but I didn't care. I felt great. Amazing even. Like I finally found something that was all mine, and didn't you just know, it lined up with something I loved anyway."

"So the bee love's been around for a long time, I take it?" Diana asked, confirming what she already knew.

"It was my first word, what do you think?" Harry asked.

"The second you graduated from a school with a dress code, you started wearing the wings and antennae with your black and yellow ensemble?"

"Got it in one," Harry said. He shrugged and took a deeper drink of coffee. "So that's it. I wear it because it makes me feel like myself, no matter what anyone else says. I mean, it still hurts when people point fun and tease, but that embarrassment and discomfort is nothing compared to how I felt before."

"Well, your subject of dress is on the unique side," Diana said, leaning up to kiss his cheek. "But it doesn't sound any weirder than the women I know who can't leave the house without a full face of make up, or the guys I know who can't function with stubble on their cheeks."

Harry blinked at her for a second, stilling.

"I'm saying it's not that weird, Harry," Diana said. She kissed him again, this time lingering for a second longer. She patted his chest though the black and yellow striped shirt he'd put back on and pressed their foreheads together. "Though I do hope in the future you can become comfortable enough with yourself that you feel great no matter what you have on."

"Thanks," Harry said.

She pecked him quickly on the lips before hopping out of the bed. Diana stretched and ruffled his hair before kissing the top of it. "Good. Now we're both about to be late for work, and we need to plan a picture date, because six year old, blue carpenter bee Harry is something I *need* to see."

Harry laughed, so gravely and warm and happy that Diana's heart skipped.

Things were just starting, weren't they?

Diana couldn't wait.

# CHAPTER 12

ARRIVING TO WORK together caused less of a stir than either of them expected.

It had felt so normal and right to finish eating breakfast with each other before piling into Diana's car to head to the mall before they were both late for work. The drive had been as pleasant as any date together, and Diana had almost forgotten where they were going if not for the morning text from Jolie reminding her to "cut the honeymoon short."

Her text back had been appropriately censored to save Harry from turning too red when he caught sight of the screen on accident.

The only thing more pleasant than the car ride to work, was being early enough that Diana didn't have to rush. She was perfectly content to stroll down the empty mall walk with her hand in Harry's. She laced their fingers together and squeezed, her heart so happy she could burst.

She'd do this every day if she could get away with it.

All the same though, good times had to end, at least for now. Diana let go of his hand as they stopped in front of the honey store. His fingers brushed hers, almost as if he wanted to grab it again, but he didn't. He kissed her on the cheek instead and bumped their foreheads together.

"Thanks for last night," Harry said. "I'm really glad Jolie dropped me off at your place."

"I'm really glad she did, too," Diana said right back.

Harry took a step back, and waved. "I'll see you later, okay?"

"Of course. And I'll pick you up after work to take you home, okay? Your car is still at your house, right?" Diana asked, looking through her bag for her work key. It was her turn to unlock the doors this morning with Jolie coming in later. "That okay?"

"I can just catch a ride home with Princess," Harry said, shoving his hands in his pockets. "You really don't have to go out of your way, especially since your store closes so much earlier than mine."

"Aw, you're ruining my plans to kidnap you and take you home again," Diana said, pulling her key out of her purse in success. "I have a whole night planned."

"Then you'll never get to see my baby pictures," Harry added.

"Jerk."

"You know I'm not."

"Are you two seriously flirting in front of the store?" Princess asked, sticking her head out of the door. Her angry glare looked forced, like she was merely holding up an act of annoyance. Diana was impressed at her dedication. Up until Princess narrowed her eyes at Harry and growled. "And where were you last night? You didn't come home from your walk!"

"That's because he stayed the night at my place," Diana said. It was when she saw Princess' face turn a brilliant shade of pink, followed by the gaping mouth that she realized she had said too much, too quickly. "Are you okay?"

"You. And he." Princess covered her mouth and pointed. "All night?"

Harry snorted into his hands, his shoulders shaking as she floundered about with her words.

Princess glared even harder and yelled. "Stop laughing you jerk and— wait. Where's the rest of your outfit?"

"Oh," Harry said. He rubbed the back of his neck and licked the side of his lips. "The wings got ripped, and my antennae headband broke."

Diana was about to save Harry the trouble of explaining he'd been beat up, surely he didn't want his younger friend to worry about him, but they were both saved by Princess' wild imagination.

"Don't tell me any more! Too much information!" She shrieked before running back into the shop, ears and face now redder than they were pink.

Now it was Harry's turn to flush and his shoulders raised in embarrassment. "I'm going to have to tell her I got beat up, aren't I?"

Diana hugged his arm and grinned. "I don't know. This is almost funnier."

"I'm going to have to tell her."

"You really shouldn't," Diana laughed. She dropped her head on his shoulder and snickered into his arm. "This is too good. My only regret is

Jolie knows the truth or I would have seen if we couldn't have got her going to."

"She would have liked it too much."

"Point."

"I'll see you after work then?" Harry asked. He hugged Diana to his side and grinned. "I'm pretty sure my ride home with Princess just got denied."

"Absolutely," Diana said. She tugged him down by his furry collar and planted a kiss on his lips. "I'll kidnap you properly this time, without Jolie's intervention."

"Looking forward to it," Harry said.

"Good," Diana said. She pressed into his side and let her face rest against the black and yellow fabric of his shirt. The fuzz from his collar tickled her forehead and everything felt so right with the world Diana felt like she was floating. She could go on like this forever. Just her and the odd man who she almost didn't give a second chance to. But oh was she glad that she did. Diana would have to think of someway to thank Jolie later.

For now, though, Diana hugged Harry's side. "It's a date."

## Acknowledgements

To God be the glory forever, and ever, Amen.

As always: Thanks to God in the highest for the talent to write, and the push He gave to everyone who inspired me, helped me, and encouraged me. And of course, thanks be to God for giving us Jesus, who loves you & me.

At this particular moment: I want to give thanks to my friend Mary! She was a huge help in taking a step outside of my usual genres, and for helping out with the first few drafts and making sure I stuck with the story, even when it refused to cooperate. And of course, I always want to give extra thanks to family and friends who helped keep me on track.

Thank you for reading!

## About The Author

Grey Liliy is a young woman who claims the East Coast of Virginia as her home. She enjoys anime, video games, movies, novels, and comics of just about any genre. Liliy has been drawing & writing a comic of her own since 2005, called *The Adventures of Wiglaf and Mordred*. Her debut novel, *Children of Hephaestus* was published in September 2012.

www.ingramcontent.com/pod-product-compliance
Lightning Source LLC
Chambersburg PA
CBHW052142220626
47052CB00005B/1163